Bye-Bye Baby

Oh God, Bry, you honestly do think you're going to live forever.

The speaker is Baby Robin Cantrell, the most famous female tennis player in the world. The person addressed is Bryant Gilchrist, her divorced husband. The occasion: an outrageous seduction attempt, by the former of the latter.

Baby *is* a terror, no question. And a charmer. And Bry is only one of a sizeable number with severely mixed feelings about her —a number that includes the well-known detecting team of Helen and Jacob Horowitz.

For the Tri-Town Invitational, the midpoint of Baby's farewell tour, an all-star international cast (with a lot of secret agendas) has assembled. Violence erupts. Helen and Jacob, smack in the middle of it all, find their lives intensified in a way that shakes them both.

Is *their* marriage as vulnerable as *ordinary* marriages when they had blithely assumed it wasn't?

by the same author

THE LAST GAMBIT
THE LIARS' LEAGUE
DEAD FACES LAUGHING
DEATH OF A NYMPH
THE NICE MURDERERS
ONE MAN'S MURDER
SUDDEN DEATH

DAVID DELMAN

Bye-Bye Baby

THE CRIME CLUB
An Imprint of HarperCollins *Publishers*

First published in Great Britain in 1992
by The Crime Club, an imprint of
HarperCollins Publishers, 77–85 Fulham Palace Road,
Hammersmith, London W6 8JB

9 8 7 6 5 4 3 2 1

David Delman asserts the moral right to be identified
as the author of this work.

© David Delman 1992

A catalogue record for this book is
available from the British Library

ISBN 0 00 232424 3

Photoset in Linotron Baskerville by
Rowland Phototypesetting Ltd
Bury St Edmunds, Suffolk
Printed and bound in Great Britain by
HarperCollins Book Manufacturing, Glasgow

All rights reserved. No part of this publication may be
reproduced, stored in a retrieval system, or transmitted,
in any form or means, electronic, mechanical,
photocopying, recording or otherwise, without the prior
permission of the publishers.

To the Reader

Worlds made by novelists are not bound to be factual.

Realism is another matter, of course.

So my world of female tennis players—and their satellites—is proof against criticism that takes the form of: 'He left out (fill in favourite notable's name).'

Martina, for instance, is nonexistent in *BYE-BYE BABY*.

Chrissy does flicker into life briefly.

That's another thing common to worlds made by novelists. They tend to be idiosyncratic.

For
Jordan Henry Forbes

PROLOGUE

The National Tennis Center, Flushing Meadows, NY
September, 1993

As they cut away for a commercial the man with the network TV emblem on his blazer turned to the woman whose blazer and emblem matched his and said, 'I hate rain delays.'

'Rain makes the flowers grow,' she said absently.

'I don't give much of a shit about flowers. What I give a shit about is my prostate.'

'Rain affects your prostate?'

'Everything affects my prostate. Should I go to the john now or what? I'm sort of in between.'

'Better go.'

'I think I'll wait.'

'So why ask? Who am I, your mama?'

He was bearded, balding, and mistakenly thought by many to be avuncular. But he was much too self-involved for even that degree of family feeling. She was bespectacled and bred-in-the-bone feisty. Feisty to her fingernails, he thought. She had lived feisty and would die feisty. He pictured her on her deathbed, feisty.

'Speaking of mamas, *hers* seems particularly pissed,' he said.

'Particularly? How can you tell?'

'You didn't see?'

'See what?'

'You didn't see her give me the finger when I waved hello?'

'Who asked you to wave hello?'

'I was being civil.'

'You're always being civil. You're a fucking civil service, you are.'

Better than always being feisty, he thought, but said, 'Hey, that's just the way I am. *My* mama raised me right.'

'*Her* mama gives *everybody* the finger. She's a thug, didn't you know? Besides, she's having fits, thinking every minute her kid's in danger of being exploited.'

'By who?'

'By whom—jeeze!'

'All right, don't *die* on me. By *whom?*'

'By her agent, by the tournament director, by the Women's International Tennis Association, for God's sake, and let's not forget you and me. Try and get a post match interview if her kid loses.'

'She promised.'

A pitying glance for his non-insider naïveté—but one in a series long enough by now for him to be inured to it. Almost.

'Her kid can take care of herself,' he said. 'Her kid looks to me like a kid who could go three sets plus fifteen rounds with the heavyweight champ. You see those thighs?'

'Appearances. That's your trouble, Skipper boy. Appearances have always—'

But they were on camera again before she could complete the insight. He leaned forward familiarly, his practised smile attractive in his tanned, ever-pleasant face.

'This is Skip Hancock welcoming you back to the US Open,' he said to the TV audience. 'Where I still can't get used to the non-sound of 747s not zooming in from Laguardia, though this is the fourth year in a row that New York's tennis buff of a mayor has persuaded the FAA to alter traffic patterns. Freddie Jo, the National Tennis Center is downright tomb-like.'

'Yes, it is, Skip. Could be we're in the middle of my native Arizona. Or your native Kansas.'

They shared a congenial laugh at this.

'Instead of beautiful, downtown Flushing Meadows,' he said. 'As you can see, we're not quite ready to resume action after our brief but brisk late summer deluge. Just about but not quite. Well, F.J., we're finally down to two.'

'Started with one hundred and twenty-eight and just two left,' she agreed, 'but an awesome twosome it is, battling for the championship and the winner's share of one of the richest tennis purses in the world. Four games each in the opening set. Couldn't be closer, could it, in this classic match-up.'

'Youth versus age.'

'Finesse versus power.'

'What do you think, F.J., will the delay give either one an edge?'

'After only eight games? Not likely. I mean, these are two superbly conditioned athletes, and anyway when you come right down to it it's *mental* toughness that matters; confidence, how they feel about themselves, how they feel about each other. In every tennis match confidence gets belted back and forth across the net as much as the ball itself. So if two players are at the same skill level it's the one latching on to more minutes of confidence who'll win.'

'How they feel about each other, you said?'

'Yes.'

'OK, how *do* they feel about each other, Freddie Jo?'

She smiled. For a moment her cat's eyes lit with malicious pleasure, but then, remembering where she was, she said, sedately enough: 'Well, they ain't friends. Everybody knows that.'

TEN MONTHS EARLIER:

BRYANT BRADSHAW GILCHRIST

CHAPTER 1

For the past three weeks Bry had been seeing 'Bye-bye Baby' posters everywhere. Various other media forms had reinforced the message. Which meant he could hardly have been unprepared for her to hit town. Which meant it was absurd of him not to be very much on guard. He knew that, even as he opened the apartment door to her distinctive point counterpoint knock—a code developed in the long-ago time when their hearts were young and gay—and allowed the enemy into the fortress.

The enemy looked wonderful. Blonde hair a bit lighter than his last view of it, golden skin a bit darker, and as for those remarkable eyes—to which no TV camera had ever done justice—they seemed, implausibly, bluer.

She wore a navy leather jacket, lightweight but expensive. She unbelted as he stepped back to permit entry, revealing a tailored white blouse and a short but dressy grey skirt. The crowd-pleasing legs were in sheer dark stockings. Baby Robin Cantrell had come a long way indeed from her 'low-life origins'—her phrase—to the point where her sense of style was not merely enviable but endemic.

She had Tommy Boswell with her. He was scowling. She was grinning. How she loved being outrageous, Bry thought.

'Hello, Bryant, my own true love,' she said and kissed him. Her arms had snaked around his neck, and her body had just begun to insinuate when he disengaged.

'Robin,' he said, nodding recognition after ten feet of buffer zone had been re-established. Nodding to Boswell, too, but not offering his hand.

Nor did Boswell offer his. He looked quite as splendid as she—hair, skin, and eyes almost a precise match, plus those Huck Finn freckles.

True Californians, the two of them. Send them around

the world year after year, and you did nothing to diminish the All-American aura. Boswell was a year or so younger than Robin, putting him at thirty-three. Not much top-flight tennis left in him either, the savants had been saying. With both of them gone, tennis would certainly be the drabber for it, Bry acknowledged.

She had been studying him. 'You've been exercising,' she said. 'You look downright athletic. Who would have thunk—Bryant Gilchrist looking outdoorsy.'

He said nothing.

'Come on, admit it. I did you some good after all.'

He smiled thinly.

'Well, I did,' she said and set off on a quick tour of the apartment. 'You could stand some paint-up, fix-up,' she said. 'I told you that bathroom was going to have to be re-done. Those shower tiles, Bry, they're a disgrace. But still, it's how I remember it, just the snuggest little first-floor walk-up ever. All books and leather chairs and stuff. I saw you being Bryant the scholar. I knocked on the window, but you pretended not to hear.'

'I *didn't* hear.'

She turned to Boswell. 'He *is* a concentrater. He's amazing that way, really. He bends over those books, and it's like he's gone somewhere.' Back to Bry. 'Where's the picture?'

'What picture?'

Again to Boswell. 'He had this trick picture of me. I don't know here he got it, but he got it, and he had it blown up. Taken three years ago—you know, the last time I won Wimbledon. During the match, during change of court. A trick of light or something because presto—I'm thirteen again and in my first big tournament. I'm sitting there in a chair, a towel around my neck, squinting up into the sun and smiling fit to glory. Bryant had a name for it. What was it, Bry?'

'I don't remember.'

'*Innocence Revisited.* How do you like that, Tommy? I mean, that's the kind of stuff you get when you marry an English teacher.'

Boswell glanced at his watch. 'Listen, is this going to take much longer?'

'Is what, dearest?'

'This. Whatever it is. Because you've got about two hundred people waiting for you at the Hilton, and I promised your sister you wouldn't be late.'

Robin appeared to take this under advisement, gazing at him fondly as she did so. The effect, though, was to make him nervous.

'You go, Tom,' she said.

'It's not me they're waiting for.'

'I'll be along.' Placing her hands on his cheeks, she imprisoned his face. 'Charm 'em for me. You know how. Tell 'em fifteen minutes.'

'Will he drive you?'

'Yes,' she said.

'No,' Bry said.

'Yes, he will,' she said and eased Boswell towards the door. 'Don't worry about it. And don't fret about it either. It's post-divorce stuff, Tommy. Niggling little odds and ends that we've been putting off and putting off, and now we've simply got to get down to cases. I mean, if Bry and I can square it away between us, there'll be that much less for the lawyers to mess up. A nuisance, sweetie, but it won't take long.'

Boswell studied the floor for a moment, as if something there might be getting ready to nip his ankle, then he gave her a curiously sardonic smile; gave Bry something enigmatic in the way of a parting glance and left.

'Tommy's an excellent coach,' she said. 'He's got me hitting that damn backhand volley with real crispness, Bry, you'd be amazed. If I'd had him a couple of years earlier maybe I wouldn't be packing it in now. Still, he can be a bit pesky.' She paused, squinting down the corridors of time. 'I truly have had bad luck with coaches.'

'What divorce stuff?' Bry asked.

'Isn't there any? I thought there was. All right, how

about the apartment? We still own it jointly, and my lawyer thinks it ought to be sold.'

'It's on the market.'

'It is?'

'I called your lawyer and told him that two weeks ago. I told him the price I was asking and how long I thought it would take to get it. He said OK and that he would convey the information to you. I guess he forgot.'

'I guess he did.'

'And I guess he also forgot to mention that I'd like the apartment keys back so I can get the condo security guards off my neck. They keep asking me how many you had duplicated. How many did you? Fifty, for your closest friends and lovers?'

'Oh, Bry.'

'All right, you tell me.'

'Two, I think. Maybe three. You know I can't keep track of stuff like that.'

'Where's yours, incidentally?'

'I lost it. Anyway, I'd have thought you'd have changed the lock. You didn't?'

'No.'

'Why not?'

'I've been busy.' Which was no answer of course, though it was in fact the answer Bry kept giving himself.

She smiled—a corner of her mouth lifting, a way she had of registering triumph. Then she crossed the room to one of the leather chairs and dropped into it, careless about her skirt. She watched to see if he was watching and he was. That pleased her, too.

'Bry . . .'

He knew that tone. In retreat from it he went to the bookcase and for luck covered the bald marble dome of William Dean Howells with his hands. Where his hands belonged, he knew, was over his own ears.

'Bry, are you listening?'

Now he got himself to the door and opened it encouragingly. 'Thanks for dropping by,' he said.

'Don't be like that. Be my sweet lover.'

'Kindest regards to Sherry. And to Aunt Win, too, when you see her. Tell her—'

She paid no attention. In part that was because his voice, having developed some shakiness along the way, was short on authority. In part *that* was because she had slipped from her jacket and was, at a snail's pace, unbuttoning her blouse. And fundamentally it was because she never had paid much attention to him when seduction was the issue.

He shut the door. He felt like an iron filing, being drawn inexorably into a field of force.

The blouse came off. With her hands on the bra clasp she paused. 'Do I do it, or do you?'

It was the complacency that got to him, that cocksureness she couldn't be bothered to hide. He was the poor fish everlastingly on the hook and ready for reeling in when she pleased. Anger surged.

She stared back coolly—not distant, interested, even sympathetic.

He struggled for equilibrium and managed to achieve it. 'Within the next two minutes one of us leaves,' he said. 'It can be me if you prefer.'

'Bryant, you just don't know how sexy that is. I mean, when you're in a temper. I mean, it changes you so. Bryant the owl becomes Bryant the . . . I don't know. Anyway it makes me tingle.'

'Everything makes you tingle.'

'Yes, and don't you love it.'

'Alley cat,' he said and handed the blouse to her. She looked at it, took it, and before he could duck, wafted it across his face inundating him in fragrance.

'Your loss,' she said. But then she stepped back and, sighing, corrected herself. 'Ours, I mean. Oh God, Bry, you honestly do think you're going to live forever.'

He turned away while she got dressed.

'I woke up this morning with this big, terrible ache for you, Bry Brad Gilchrist. Bigger than I ever thought it would get to be. You're such a lovely lover. Well, you can thank me for that, too, can't you? *Can't* you? I mean, you'd never say you didn't need teaching once upon a time.'

He kept silent.

'What's the name of the Greek guy who took charge of the Greek lady and made her terrific?'

'Pygmalion.'

'I'm a female Pygmalion. Come on, Bry, it hasn't been all bad. We had some gorgeous times, admit it.'

He consulted his watch.

'Two years,' she said. 'Outside of tennis and my marriage to you I've hardly ever done anything that lasted two years.' She'd been applying lipstick. Now she shifted position so that it was his reflection she studied in the mirror. She nodded. 'Downright cute,' she said. 'Damned if you're not. You probably owe that to me, too. Sherry's got this king-sized crush on you, did you know that?'

'That's ridiculous.'

'Is it? Why? Because she clams up? Sherry's always been like that. I mean, from the time she got out of diapers. She figures if she hides what she wants nobody'll guess, and so nobody'll take it away from her.'

'Nobody?'

Her smile wavered, but it was impossible for him to tell how much of that was performance. 'All right, me. Sherry thinks . . . well, never mind about that. Anyway you know what Sherry thinks. You know what everybody thinks, don't you, Golden Brain. Except maybe your own complicated self. Right now, for instance. You think you want me to go, but the fact is, you don't. And if it wasn't for all those scaredy-cat Puritans in your bloodline you could kick loose, and we'd have some fun. Boy, do I have your number.'

'Waiting for me on my desk is this really extraordinary pile of work.'

'OK, OK,' she said and reached up as if to grab something out of the air. Whatever it was, she then tucked into the opening of her blouse. 'I got the message.' She shrugged. 'Win some, lose some. Listen, I'll take your car and leave it in the Hilton parking lot. You grab a cab and pick the car up later. Parking ticket will be in an envelope at the lobby desk. I'll also leave a ticket for the luncheon. Will you come?'

'No.'

'I'll leave it anyway.'

'Don't.' But after only a brief hesitation he gave her his car keys.

'Bry . . .'

'What?'

She made a clown's mournful face. 'Just like that, I'm an old lady. Did you ever think I would be? I mean I'm making farewell appearances, for God's sake. No more Wimbledons. No more any of that good stuff. All, all gone. How am I going to cope?'

He looked at her. Was there the remotest possibility that the mask camouflaged real feeling? How would he know? How would she, for that matter?—acting being as natural to her by now as her legendary backhand.

'And I'm broke, too. All that lovely money pissed away. Bry, I made damn close to six million in my time. Sherry just figured it out for me. All pissed away. I never could pick a horse. Or anything else, really, that could make money behave.' She grinned suddenly, in a way that once would have buckled his knees. Prudently he turned away from her, deflecting the impact. Even so, there was a suspicious shakiness. He swore at himself.

'But what the hell, it was a gorgeous ride, wasn't it? And I did do one thing smart. I picked a good man to marry. I should never have left you.'

'Left me?'

'You know what I mean.'

'As in I threw you out on discovering Tom Boswell had been sharing our bed?'

A faint wrinkle appeared between her brows, indicating disdain for obsessive detailing. 'Whatever.'

Jacket buttoned now, she did a last, fast check in the mirror. Something she saw amiss caused her to dig a comb from her purse and run it through her hair. 'You won't come to the luncheon?'

'No.'

'But you'll be at the Field House tomorrow night, of course.'

'Not possible. One of my students—'

She turned. 'I'll lose if you're not there,' she said. 'Why would you try to hurt me that way?'

Volumes wanted to rush out in answer, but she held up a hand to forestall him, a traffic cop's hand, which he found himself obeying.

'I know that sounds silly and superstitious, and you hate it when I get that way, but it's true. It just is. I had this dream last night. Wimbledon. At least I think it was. Anyway, grass. Hattie Lockridge's big serve. She kicks it wide to the forehand, you know? A rocket. *Real* wide, so I have to dig like mad to get there. And in this dream I do get there—in plenty of time, only as I'm levelling off for the return, my feet give out from under me. Boom! Flat on my ass. And now here's the thing—a parade of people, trainers, coaches, friends, my Aunt Win, my sister Sherry, an *army* can't get me back on my feet. Sweat, strain, nothing. And then from out of nowhere, there you are, and you just reach out your hand like from heaven. Up I go. Not only that, but there's the ball still waiting for me, and I crush it. A winner. Cross-court, untouchable. What do you think, Bry?'

'That you're being childish. Dreams are only dreams. And of course, they never mean what they seem to mean.'

'What does this one mean?'

'Probably that you're trying to swindle me out of something.'

She turned back to stare at her reflected face. 'Everybody says Hattie will be lucky to take a game from me. Bullshit! That just shows how tennis-ignorant they all are. Hattie's talented and getting better by the minute, and let's don't forget those sixteen-year-old legs. Also, she's got it in for me and for Vera Menchicov. I mean, she really hates our guts because of that dirty trick Vera played on her. All right, we both played on her, but it was Vera's stupid idea.'

'What dirty trick?'

'You know. You must know. It was locker-room talk all last year.'

'Locker-room talk is like faculty lounge talk. I despise both and never listen. It's amazing how little you ever bothered to understand about me.'

'Bry, be nice.'

'All those people at the Hilton, waiting so patiently. Surely, such patience . . .'

She returned her comb to her purse, using the moment to get thoughts in order. He watched her, trying to ready himself for whatever snare she was setting.

'The thing is, Bry dearest, Hattie will be after blood. She wants to blast me out of my very own Tri-Towns. God, to lose in the Tri-Towns' first round! I don't think I could stand that.'

The Tri-Towns Invitational, in its third year now, was co-sponsored by the municipality and by Walker University, the small, though respected liberal arts institution that employed Bry in its English Department. But it was, in fact, Robin's tournament, a concept dreamed up by her (in order to be near her one true love) and duly put into effect by Sherry, her sister-manager. In those newlywed days of romantic attachment (and sexual haze) how story-book perfect it had seemed—the bride as heroine, scoring smashing victories over arch-rival Vera Menchicov in both finals.

As pro tournaments went, of course, the Tri-Towns was an anomaly: only four women invited to compete for prize money that was modest indeed. Still, efficiently managed by Sherry, it generated a handy sum for Walker's female athletic programme, as well as a respectable amount of positive press for all concerned.

Now the Tri-Towns would become history, but it would end with a bang, having taken on extra dimension because of its position on Robin's farewell tour: Charleston, Washington, DC, the Tri-Towns (the exact midpoint), Philadelphia, Boston, and *finis*.

Robin had moved to the window, but he knew she wasn't really seeing anything that might be part of that October night. 'Actually,' she said, 'I haven't much enjoyed this farewell tour of Sherry's. Have you kept up?'

'No.'

'Bry, how come you never learned the value of a sweet lie?'

He kept silent.

Folding her hands in prayer, she placed them under her chin. 'No more fighting, please,' she said. 'The last thing I want to do is fight with you. It's like all my friends are turning against me. Vera, that Russian bitch, has chilled me twice to now, love and love in Charleston. I keep telling her—Vera, baby, Wimbledon was June. This is October. What the hell does she care? Press her button, and out she comes rushing the net. Say you'll be there, Bry. I couldn't bear it if you weren't.'

'I'll see.'

'Not I'll see—yes!' She made it across the room to him in three swooping strides. 'Please, please say yes.' Grabbing his hand, she pressed kisses all over it.

He wrenched free, back-pedalling hurriedly.

But as usual she surprised him. Instead of continuing the assault, she set about preparing to leave. She put on her jacket, belted it, collected her purse, and, having blown him a final kiss, shut the door briskly behind her. But when he listened for retreating footsteps he heard nothing. A moment later the door opened again, hesitantly.

'I just want you to know something,' she said.

'I'm not interested. I'm busy. I have papers to—'

'Listen to me, Bry. It's important, and if you'll give me a chance to say it you'll think so, too. Are you listening?'

'Go ahead.'

'I mean really.'

'I'm listening, I'm listening, I swear I'm listening.'

'What I am is a good-natured slut. Always was, always will be. But if I *could* love a man . . . one man . . . it would be you. That's for the record. Do you believe me?'

'Yes,' he said bitterly.

CHAPTER 2

She was gone. Bry had an hour yet before his Henry James seminar, which was in Swansea Hall—on the main campus as opposed to the annexe—and only a fifteen-minute walk away. He went into the kitchen for coffee. He found his favourite extra large, extra solacing mug, and poured. His hand shook. He watched it without surprise. No one, ever, had been able to attack his nerve centre the way Robin could. Due to her, he was in a condition of chronically altering states: tense and volatile with her on the scene; temperate and reasonably self-controlled with her elsewhere.

In fact, it was fair to say he had led two existences: thirty-six years of quiet—well, relative quiet—before setting eyes on her; a storm-tossed three and a half with her as a factor. Disproportionate as those periods obviously were, they managed, mysteriously, to seem of equal length.

She had his number, she had said. True enough once, no question. Did she still? His hand raising the mug had not quite recovered steadiness. Was that his answer? But he had put up a fight just now, a more vigorous one than either of them might have predicted. Was *that* his answer? In other words, could he point to progress and infer a cure? He tried hard to be swayed by the logic of it, but theirs was a relationship not friendly to logic. Randomness was their *leitmotif*, improbability their linchpin.

Sipping coffee, he sat there studying his hand and waiting for the tremor to disappear. And contemplating the ways in which he and Robin represented separate species.

Hyperbole aside, they really did have remarkably little

in common. He came from a long line of New Englanders, careful Massachusetts folk and non-venturing Vermonters. She exuded California, the essence of which appeared to be, in her case, a kind of Ariel-like waywardness. She flitted and floated, coming to earth only when she saw something she wanted, at which point she snapped it up like a bird of prey, restricted by no laws other than those of her nature.

He was Groton and Harvard. She was John Wayne High School, at least for three years, an educative interval that had ended abruptly when tournament money began rolling in.

He was reclusive by temperament, at home in libraries and seminar rooms. Even lecture halls were something of a stretch for him. She adored crowds, and they her. He had sat in a box at the US Open, marvelling at what travelled back and forth between Robin and her eroticized fans. There wasn't a man, he thought despairingly, who wasn't held in thrall by her titillating costumes and pretty legs.

Blame it all on a balky hotel elevator—Cambridge, Mass., three summers earlier. Bry was there for a weekend conference of the regional Jamesian society of which he was a newly elected board member; Robin on a break from Virginia Slims to visit Harvard's coach, an old friend and team-tennis mate. A localized power failure, afflicting one elevator on the east side of the hotel building. Robin and Bry, the only passengers, were marooned for upwards of two hours.

Actually, he hadn't even noticed her when she got on. He'd been reading, deep in his notes of the committee meeting he had just attended. His floor was the twelfth, hers the ninth. Between the sixth and seventh the elevator lurched to a violent stop. She ricocheted off him, knocking papers from his hand and his glasses to the floor.

'Holy hell,' she said.

In that dry, pseudo-upper-class English the Gilchrists had always adopted to hide panic, he diagnosed for her what they might be facing—correctly, as it turned out—

while she bent to recover book and glasses. She then looked at her watch.

'I've got an exhibition in thirty minutes,' she said.

He'd had no idea, then, what such an exhibition might entail. Nor did he ask her. Instead he went to the phone and dialled the emergency number. A concerned female voice informed him that the problem was already known to the hotel authorities and that they were working on it. An uncomfortable pause followed, after which the voice reminded them that it *was* Sunday and that rescue might be 'just a wee bit' delayed.

'Sir?'

'Yes?'

'May I have your name?' Bry told her. 'Are there ... others?'

He turned to Robin. 'It seems we may be here for a while, and the hotel people would like your name.'

Her eyes widened. He supposed that was the moment he first realized how remarkable they were. 'You don't know it?' she asked.

She had, in fact, begun to look familiar, but after a period of fruitless inner search he confessed his ignorance. 'Sorry, no. Are you an actress? I don't get to the movies as often as I'd like. Or the theatre,' Bry had time to add since she was involved in an intense—and apparently endless—scrutiny of him. 'Or watch much TV, for that matter.'

She took the phone. 'Robin Cantrell,' she said into it. 'And I've got a match on in twenty minutes.' Without waiting for an answer, she hung up. Turning back to Bry, she said, 'You're not bad-looking for a hermit. Except you're so skinny and pale. Like a corpse. Don't you ever get out of doors at all? You don't, do you?'

'In the summers I swim sometimes.'

'But not this summer.'

'No,' he admitted.

Suddenly she reached forward the thumb and index finger of her right hand and tweaked his upper arm. 'What do you do for biceps when you need them? Borrow somebody's?'

Startled, he stepped back heedlessly enough to bang his head against the elevator wall.

'You OK?'

He felt so utterly foolish that he forgot to be properly Gilchristy. 'Yes. Of course,' he said. 'It's just that I'm not used to . . .'

She watched with interest while he floundered and then, after a fashion, came to his rescue.

'You're not used to being touched?'

He nodded.

'By women, you mean.'

He cleared his throat, which she construed as an assent.

'I see,' she said thoughtfully.

It was as if she were now in possession of an odd fact, not quite startling enough to be incredible but certainly constituting a kind of esoterica.

After a moment she said, 'Actually, I'm as skinny as you are, but I'm also wiry and strong. Here, feel.' She brought his hand to one of her own superbly developed biceps. 'I'm that way all over,' she said when she saw he had taken note. 'Not just another pretty face, according to Sammy Edwards in this morning's *Boston Globe*, but a perfectly proportioned tennis machine. "Baby Robin, the giant-killer," that's what he called me. You don't read the sports pages?'

'Not often.'

'Ever?'

'Well, no.'

'What *do* you read, mouldy old library books?'

'Mostly.'

Like a lepidopterist seeking the precise Latin nomenclature to fit his category, she pondered him, eyes narrowed, brow wrinkled. 'And I bet you write poetry,' she said suddenly.

'No. That is, not any more. I used to.'

'I thought so.'

'But that was a long time ago.'

'So what do you do now?'

He told her.

'I bet your girl students think you're cute. You almost are, once a person gets used to the skinniness. And the shyness. Actually shy people sort of turn me on. Probably that's because I don't know any, except maybe Sherry, my sister, and she's not so much shy as quiet.' She paused and shook her head. 'I thought everybody knew who I was. You really *didn't* recognize me?'

'No, but I think I do now.'

'Who am I?'

'A professional tennis player,' he said, then amplified hurriedly. 'An internationally famous one.'

She smiled. 'Not bad. The most famous female tennis player in the world would have been better.'

'Are you?'

'Well, of course I am,' she said, mildly exasperated. 'God, for a college professor you certainly are uninformed. OK, might as well kill time one way as another. Take a load off.'

He was hauled down and positioned so that they were shoulder to shoulder on the elevator floor. 'Easy does it there. I'm not going to eat you, just educate you. What was that name again?'

He repeated it.

'Bryant,' she said reflectively. 'Family name?'

'My mother's.'

'Bryant. Sort of cold and distant, isn't it? Bry's cosier. Pay attention to teacher, Bry, or get your knuckles cracked, understood?'

He nodded.

At once she began an uninhibited—and unexpurgated —version of her autobiography. He was fascinated.

Just the two daughters in that ill-starred family. Their father had been a police officer, gunned down in his early thirties by a berserk drug addict—their mother the lovely but highstrung girl who'd been his childhood sweetheart. A year after Pete Cantrell's death, Kate Cantrell had taken her own life.

'I was ten,' Robin said matter-of-factly. 'But already on my way to becoming an LA street kid. Sherry was eight, and don't ask me where she was heading. I have no idea. I wasn't home that much.

'Anyway along comes Aunt Win, my dad's older sister, and we got whisked out of LA to this place you never heard of. Brunswick, Georgia? I didn't think so. She had a few bucks, Aunt Win did. Not a lot, but what you could put away if you were a very careful-living schoolteacher and had no husband or kids or anything to spend your money on.

'She saved our lives, I guess.' She paused. 'I've spent damn near twenty-five years hating her guts, old hatchet-face.' She turned to study him. 'I bet you're the kind who thinks that's impossible, hating a person even though she saved your life. I bet you're just wild about your dear old mom.'

'I was, as a matter of fact, quite fond of her. She's dead now.' And then, before he knew he was going to, added: 'It was my father I detested.'

'Why?'

'He deserved it.'

'What's the worst thing he ever did to you?'

He kept silent.

She punched his shoulder, not at all gently. 'Come on, Bry, how else are we going to be friends? Friends tell each other stuff, secret stuff. That's how they know they're friends. It's like a ceremony, like what the Indians do. Mixing blood?'

'You are the most amazing person,' he said.

'I'm waiting.'

He spent some time shifting nervously from one haunch to the other and then found himself saying, 'It was the way he punished me. No matter what the crime—and they were never really major, I was a well-behaved little boy—I'd be locked in the closet. It was a cellar closet, very small, very dark.' He paused to wet his lips before continuing. 'Locked in the closet for never less than an hour, and once for an entire afternoon. Pretty soon I learned not to cry. Crying only extended the punishment.' He stared at the floor.

After a while she took his hand. 'A real bad-ass,' she said. 'Bet he was a cowpoke, too.'

He looked at her blankly. 'He was a physicist.'

'Don't be dumb. A cowpoke! You never heard the term? Pokes cows, women. Bet he was. That kind of bad-ass usually is.'

He was silent a moment. 'What I know for certain is that he was a drunk.' He tried to stop there but found he couldn't. 'And a miser. He paid for my schooling. Aside from that he kept us—my mother and me—at just above subsistence level. And yet—' But now he did make himself break off.

'Even bet I know the "and yet". People liked him. People thought he was a sweetie-pie. Jesus, Bry, you're looking at me like I'm some kind of genius.'

'You do seem to grasp things quickly.'

'Anybody . . . everybody knows about masks. And the icky stuff that gets hidden behind them. Where on earth have you been?'

'Cloistered, I suppose.'

Her gaze swept over him, inventorying. 'Maybe you need someone like me to smarten you up, make a project out of you. What do you think?' But before he could answer she said, 'The old man's dead, too?'

'Yes.'

'But you've got his money, right?'

'Yes.'

'Was there a lot?'

'Enough. And every now and then I spend some of it in ways I know he'd hate.'

She grinned. 'Bry holds grudges. You do have a surprise or two in you, don't you, Bry?'

To defray further probing—she had less hesitancy before the personal question than anyone he'd ever met—he asked, quickly, 'Is your aunt still alive?'

'Yeah, she's alive.' She glanced away from him, down

the length of her trousered legs. She wore a thin white blouse that revealed tantalizing glimpses of satin and lace and bright yellow linen slacks. These seemed suddenly to require study. When finally she spoke her voice was dry and her gaze distant.

'The thing about Win is her sense of duty. Once she fixes on it, clear out of her way or she'll stomp you to death. She was in Italy, in Florence, on her summer holiday when the news reached her that mom had knocked herself off. She grabbed the next plane to LA, because just like that she had her vocation: a couple of baby Cantrells to save from themselves. We were going to get moulded, and she was going to be there to see it done right or kill us trying.' She paused. 'If it hadn't been the tennis, it for damn sure would have been something else.'

The tennis. At a local playground, pure accident had put a racket in Robin's hand. She'd been in charge of Sherry that morning, taking her for a walk around the perimeter of the court area, tormenting and teasing her out of resentment for the task. A player (a boy, thirteen, fourteen) having missed a shot, flung his racket in frustration. The racket head struck Sherry's head, felling her dramatically.

Convinced he was a murderer, the boy had fled in panic. A half-hour later, at a different playground, Sherry—pressing a coin against the bruised area to hold down swelling—watched while Robin hit her first forehands off a practice wall.

'Hooked,' Robin said. 'Love at first sight, almost. Not just the action of it, not just the way your body feels running and hitting. And not just the winning either, but the prettiness, too. I mean the line of flight when you hit the ball square. I still love it, always will. And you have no idea what I'm talking about, do you?'

'Actually, I think I do.'

'Do you?'

'What you're talking about, it seems to me, is passion. I don't think that's confined to tennis.'

'Do you have passions, Bry?'

'I do.'
'Name one.'
'Nineteenth-century American literature.'
For a moment she was silent. Then she doubled over in soundless laughter.

But somehow he was not offended. 'It strikes me your aunt might be a person of passion, too,' he said.

The laughter cut off. 'You think so?'

He nodded.

'Well, you're right. Me. That was her passion.'

'Not your sister?'

'Mostly me. Sherry got off just about scot-free thanks to me. Passion? Yeah, I guess so. Old Win had a four-word motto when I was growing up. From the time I was ten I must have heard it five-thousand times. Very simple: "Best in the world." And what it meant was very simple, too: work till you drop.'

It was a week or so after the racket-throwing incident that Robin's aunt had first become involved.

'In the way she always could she sniffed it out that something was up, and one day tracked me to the playground, watching from behind some bush or something. All of a sudden she pops out and grabs a racket from this innocent bystander—grabs it right away from this little black girl—and drags me kicking and screaming from the practice board to the court.

'There were kids on it; she shooed them off, told them their time was up, and if they didn't skedaddle she'd call the cops.

'For the next hour she ran my butt all over creation. I mean she was never much better than a low-grade club player, one step up from hacker, but what the hell, I was only ten.

'When we finished, she motioned me over to the net and said, "You need a teacher." No smile. Nothing joyous about it, you understand. Or prideful. Or giving me any credit. Not that way at all, but like the voice of doom: "You need a teacher."

'Two weeks later I started lessons. Six months after that she shut down the house in Brunswick, and we're back in California.'

Small and scrawny, Robin at ten had been jack-rabbit quick. And to all intents and purposes tireless. Tireless at practice. And tireless in competition, able to wear down better players late in their matches.

By her thirteenth birthday she was already a consistent winner—all the way to the quarter-finals in the US Open. Wimbledon semis the following year, with the commensurate lofty ranking: seventh in the world.

But at sixteen precocity suddenly caught up to itself, and she began losing. Before long panic set in, then depression. The tailspin steepened. It was then Win sought out J. T. Ramirez.

'Ramirez?' Robin's eyebrows formed interrogatory Vs.

Bry shook his head apologetically.

She sighed for his ignorance. 'You're even worse off than I thought. Boy, have we got stuff to work on.'

He mumbled something he knew she would find unintelligible.

'Come again?'

'Pity there are time constraints,' he said.

'Such as?'

'One day they will liberate us.'

'And so?'

He swallowed but said nothing. The notion that 'we' might have a life transcending the elevator's difficulties tied his tongue and reddened his cheeks. If she noticed, she pretended not to.

'That's J for Juan and T for Tomás, but everyone calls him Jatie. All he ever did was win back to back US Opens and then retire to become the absolute best coach in the business. Jatie saw the trouble right away, my backhand. I wasn't strong enough, you see, to really zing it the way champions have to. So, basically, what he did was switch me to the two-hander, which Chrissy was already killing people with.' She paused. 'Chris Everett.' She said the name slowly as if to someone either very foreign or mentally impaired. 'It can't be you don't know who she is? I mean, that's like not knowing the name of the President of the United States.'

He hadn't sunk that low. In possession of the surname now he could and did, in a manner of speaking, identify the Chrissy in question. Robin nodded cautious approval and continued.

'For a while it was sheer hell. It was like I was Miss Stumblebum, USA. Everybody was beating me. Girls I used to take in straight sets were putting me away. But Jatie kept me working, kept telling me if I didn't give up I'd win Wimbledon that year.

'And I did. I beat Chris for the cup, my first of four. Not that it means much to the likes of you, but four Wimbledons is something to write home about. You know how many women have won four Wimbledons?'

'No,' he said humbly.

'You wouldn't.'

'But I'm sure it must be an entirely negligible number.'

She smiled, mollified. 'OK, so that was Wimbledon' seventy-six. I was seventeen. And after that it was me and Chris and then the rest of the world, until Vera came along. Now Chrissy's gone. Vera's catching up, but I've got just the bit of an edge.

'Vera Menchicov,' he said quickly.

She stared. 'Wonders will never cease.'

'I happened to see her being interviewed on television last night.'

'What did she say?'

He struggled to remember. 'She said she came here from Moscow when she was fifteen, which was the first time she ever saw a tennis racket.'

'That's one of her favourite fairytales. She wants everyone to think she's got this marvellous natural talent. Actually, she came here when she was twelve. And both her parents were players, decent ones for Russians. Did she say that thing about speaking seven languages?'

'Yes.'

'Another fairytale. She speaks two. One and a half. She's forgotten most of her Russian. What else did she say?'

'That you're her best friend.'

She grinned. 'Well, that's for real, I guess. You think she's beautiful?'

He nodded.

'Pretty as I am?'

As if pent up too long, the words broke free and tossed their hats in the air. 'I don't think anyone is.'

She looked at him gaugingly. 'The issue is what's fair,' she said with seeming irrelevance. But since it was not the first time during this implausible conversation that he'd had difficulty keeping up, he waited, having gleaned by now that patience might be rewarded. 'What the issue really comes to, I guess, is are we going to have a thing?'

Witchcraft had turned him to stone.

'Because if we are then maybe you have to be warned.'

He said nothing.

She sighed. 'I guess you're the last person I ought to ask. If we're going to have one it's strictly up to me, isn't it?' She leaned forward then and kissed him for the first time. It was a lingering but gentle kiss. Such a quiet, laid-back kiss to cause his head to spin and his ears to go up in flames.

'Well, well,' she said and at once put a mini-chasm between them.

Bry reached to bring her back, but she eluded him. 'Jatie,' she said firmly.

The several deep breaths he took had some effect.

'The thing is I ditched him right after I won the US Open that year. I had to. It was time. Mind you, I gave him a potful of money, which he drank, gambled or whored away. But he's Vera's coach now, so pretty soon he should be OK again, financially at least. Still, I *did* ditch him, and Jatie can be weird.'

'Weird?'

'Well, violent. He has this temper, always has had. He goes along, goes along being just ordinary Jatie, a pussycat actually, and then he'll get this bee in his bonnet and explode. He put a young man in the hospital recently. We hushed it up, but it cost a little. We being Vera and me.'

'He's Vera's coach, but he still wants you?'

'Not really. It's Vera he's crazy about these days, but Jatie in a temper can get . . .'

'What?'

'Confused. Or maybe he just doesn't really care that much about sorting things out. I don't know. It's too complicated for my little brain. That particular young man happened to fancy me, as a matter of fact. Vera hardly knew him. Jatie kicked him and broke three of his ribs. Later he apologized. Muttered something about having made a mistake.'

After a moment Bry said, 'Will it surprise you to hear I'm not a physical coward?'

'Nope.'

'It won't?'

'Pale and skinny doesn't necessarily mean gutless. I know that. Actually, you give me the feeling of someone who could get himself fairly well battered and bruised on account of not being sensible. Which is really all I've been trying to warn against.' She reached across to touch his cheek. 'I mean, I wouldn't like it if you got battered and bruised.'

He caught her hand. And, having mustered courage, was about to kiss the fingers of it when she snatched it away. 'There's this other reason I told you about Jatie,' she said. 'Which is so you should know about *me*. Stop looking at my tits for a moment and listen up. Oh, for heaven's sake, I *like* you looking at my tits . . . I just want you concentrating. Are you?'

He said yes, but she had to shake him a bit before deciding it was worthwhile proceeding.

'What you should know is, I ditch people,' she said. 'It's not that I want to. And I swear it's not that I'm basically a mean person. It's just that sooner or later I always do. Bry, I could hurt you.'

'Could you?'

'Damn it, I mean this to be taken seriously, and you're not listening. All you want to do is grab hold of me.'

He inched towards her.

For another moment she held him off, expression closed, Cassandra intent on prophesying. But nothing came of it. Instead she let her body go soft, flexible, and fall into his arms. 'As if we had any choice,' she said.

'None,' he said, acutely conscious of having reached the apex of his life.

Married in a month, they'd been divorced in twenty-six.

CHAPTER 3

Helen Horowitz opened the door for Bry and then raced back into her kitchen to forestall a scorched chop, she explained over her shoulder. 'There's martini junk in the living-room.'

He found the fixings on the bar, made use of them and then dropped into an old frump of a chair, which seemed to smile at him as if longing for company. He realized suddenly how tired he was. Recently, he had become a jogger and was proficient enough now to go three miles a day, four days a week without feeling more than usefully exercised. Physical fatigue simply wasn't in it with the emotional kind, he decided. He sipped the martini gratefully, letting that and his surroundings solace him.

While the Horowitz apartment missed opulence by a considerable distance, it hit comfortable dead centre, and he always liked being in it. It ran to big unfashionable furniture—befitting the Horowitzes themselves—thick carpets, lots of shelving for books and interesting clusters of photographs, mostly of people, a few of whom were startlingly famous. You could feel protected here, he thought, a cocoon of civilization, though with just that degree of clutter to suggest the next size up in apartments would have been exactly right. He had once asked Helen if she'd considered that.

'I have,' she said, 'but I think it might wreck my marriage. I mean, money wouldn't be a problem any more because we're both doing pretty well, but every time I hint at making some kind of move Jacob goes ape. He hates new things.'

What they were both doing pretty well at in their respective ways was the business of law and order. Jacob was a homicide lieutenant in the Tri-Towns police department. Leaving it at that, however, would be understating to the point of distortion. He was what was called a 'hot-copy cop', which acknowledged the fact that over the years he had been brilliantly successful in a series of sensational murder cases.

From time to time New York City, only 30 miles from the Tri-Towns, sent siren songs wafting his way. A career path in The Apple, the lyrics went, would be considerably more rewarding in terms of money and prestige. Jacob agreed but stayed put. As Helen said, he hated new things.

Helen also insisted that Jacob was innately lazy.

'Not about everything, you understand. He does have his dervish days. But I tell you, Bry, laziness is what explains the way he lets himself be pushed around here. The fact that he hasn't made captain is an outrage. Mayor Knudsen and the quintet of jealous slobs he calls Township Council turn green *en masse* at the mere mention of his name. They play these nasty little "Get Jacob" games, at which he's more or less amused and I more or less go crazy.'

Nothing could have kept Helen, a born entrepreneur, on the township payroll indefinitely, but it was this scandalous Jacob-bashing that had triggered her departure—a shade prematurely—three years earlier. Until then she'd been something of a hot-copy cop herself, in the department's Juvenile Branch. Now she had an increasingly profitable private investigation business, successful enough to require two full-time operatives and to have twice attracted merger offers from much larger firms.

She came in from the kitchen, bearing a plate of hard pretzels which she set down next to him. Five-nine, broad-shouldered, full-breasted, narrow-waisted, she was a woman men looked at and were drawn to. Jacob, to whom this magnetism was not an unalloyed pleasure, had told Bry once that it seemed to be stronger now in her mid-forties than it had been ten years ago.

'It's that damn Apache heritage,' he said. 'Her great-grandfather was a tribal shaman, you see, and he passed down a supply of love philtres to the women of that family. Don't tell *me* he didn't. Her mother was the same damn way.'

It was the first part of that that stuck in Bry's mind—the shaman part. He never doubted it.

She had a helmet of dark hair, dark eyes, and the smooth, dark skin that, along with high cheekbones could also be traced to an Apache source.

'Only one-eighth,' Helen enjoyed saying, 'but it wears warpaint.'

Basically sunny, she had a way of going distant at times, and people who knew her best tended to leave her to Jacob until they felt safe with her again. Bry liked her tremendously. He was delighted—and always a little surprised—to realize that she liked him.

'The man called just before you got here,' she said. 'He'll be an hour or so late, and we're to have dinner without him. They got a confession out of Kearney, you know.'

Kearney was the serial rapist-killer who for the past three months had terrorized the population of both New York City and the Tri-Towns. An *ad hoc* team, headed by Jacob, and made up of specialists from both police forces, had caught him earlier in the week.

'Heard it on the car radio. I was surprised. I guess I thought of him as the kind who'd never confess, who'd insist on playing it out.'

'Your trouble is, you don't know how good Jacob is at his job.'

Yes, he thought. Or, to put it more accurately, it was

something he *had* known but in a disengaged, inactive way. Now for some reason perspective shifted, and he experienced an inexplicable—certainly misplaced—moment of sympathy for the hunted, undeserving though he was.

'What's wrong?' Helen asked.

'Nothing. Someone just walked on my grave, I guess.'

'Anyway, he's got a bit of wrapping up to do before he leaves the office.' She looked at Bry and grinned. 'He'll be tough to beat tonight. Full of beans and aggressive as hell. So watch yourself OTB.'

OTB—Over the (Chess)Board—was where Jacob and he had met; over the board at the Tri-Towns Chess Club a year and a half ago. It was a small club, composed of only 23 members who gathered once a week. That seemed to satisfy the rest, but it left Jacob and Bry with whetted appetites. As a consequence they had arranged a home and home series, alternating Wednesdays when possible.

If Bry was the more experienced player, Jacob was the more natural one. That is, the former knew theory, the latter—Bry acknowledged—had the bolder imagination. It made for stimulating, always unpredictable competition.

Over and above the games themselves, however, there was a heritage factor to add an interesting complication. They discovered they were second generation opponents. Their fathers had been fellow members of the Manhattan Chess Club, America's oldest. And in the glorious (or bizarre) year—which is to say the year Bry's fixated father had suddenly transported his family from Weymouth, Massachusetts to New York City so that he could be near the club, and two years before booze became absolute king in his life—Horowitz and Gilchrist, having battled to a series of draws, shared the club's championship. So that Jacob and Bry had grown up knowing vaguely of each other's existences.

'Bryant Bradshaw Gilchrist, are you there? Come in, BBG.'

He started, becoming aware that Helen had been repeating his name. 'Sorry.'

She was seated on the sofa. Now she put her feet up on the coffee table and sipped from her martini. 'Tough day with America's young?' she asked.

'Not really.'

'No,' she said.

He looked at her. 'My former wife is in town.'

'Yes,' she said. 'I saw her. With a couple of her tennis chums as they were leaving Township Hall, where I believe Mayor Knudsen had just given her the Tri-Towns key.' Pause. 'She looked terrific.'

'Yes.'

Another pause. 'It's none of my business, of course.'

'What isn't? My colourful domestic life? Maybe not. Only I keep remembering that on that night of all nights when I broke in here stinking drunk you didn't boot me out.'

'Jacob wouldn't let me.'

'It wasn't Jacob who cleaned up the mess I made on the living-room floor, then cleaned me up and put me to bed. In my view that gives you certain inalienable rights if you want to exercise them, though I'm not sure why you would.'

She studied him for an extended moment. 'I sometimes wonder what kind of little boy you were.'

'Do you? Why?'

'Because the so-called grown-up takes such pleasure in seeing himself through the wrong end of the telescope.'

'I thought I was getting over that.'

'Not fast enough,' she said unsympathetically.

He smiled. 'What kind of little boy was I? Lonely. My father was a famous drunk and my mother a famous tramp. As you might imagine, they led very full lives.'

'Is that for real?'

'They were the Scott and Zelda Fitzgerald of their set. Among the high-steppers of Weymouth, Mass., they were absolutely pre-eminent, each with a special claim. My father never saw a bottle he didn't like. And my poor, sweet, silly mother never saw a bed she didn't.'

'Ah, Bry.'

They were silent a moment. 'Which tennis chums?' he asked. 'Boswell and Ramirez?'

'I've seen them only on TV and am not sure I'd know them. There were two men, though. And two women. I recognized Vera Menchicov, who's at least twice as striking off camera as on. God, she's tall, Bry, even taller than I am. Could the other have been Robin's sister?'

'Yes.'

'She was never a player?'

'She quit young.'

'Why am I not surprised?'

He glanced at her.

'Don't ask me to explain that,' Helen said, 'because I can't. Except I've got this feeling that if Robin Cantrell were my older sister, I'd have a *history* of quitting things. Robin gave me a big hug and a kiss. I wanted to belt her.'

'Instead you hugged and kissed back.'

'More or less. At any rate I stood still for it.'

'Irresistible, isn't she?'

'Well, I wouldn't go that far.' He thought Helen was looking at him now as if they'd reached a point she'd had in mind to begin with. 'But you would?'

'I don't know.'

'What does that mean?'

He shut his eyes. At once he saw red streaks beneath the lids. They turned into tiny semaphore flags and started sending him messages, but the code was one he couldn't read. When he opened his eyes Helen was swinging the foot of a crossed leg impatiently.

'The attack was repulsed today,' he said, 'but I'd never swear the enemy was defeated.'

Her foot stopped swinging. She sat straight and still, concentrated, in a way that suggested the magic-making ancestor ascribed to her by Jacob. 'Voracious damn bitch,' she said softly. 'Little Miss Available Ass, ready to lift her skirt for anything that moves.'

'Why don't you put a spell on her?'

She didn't smile. Her face seemed to darken. And

lengthen. But after a moment she sighed heavily and stood up. 'Dinner,' she said. 'We'll eat in the kitchen. Give me five minutes. Hit the bathroom if you want to.'

'Helen . . .'

She waited.

'The truth is she can't help herself much,' he said.

'Wrong, Bry. Just because the damn itch is there doesn't mean one has to roll over and assume the position.'

'It's different with you.'

'With me? Is that who we're talking about?'

'I thought it might be,' he said.

'All right, if it is, here's a flash for you. It's *not* different. The itch is universal. I'll put it plainer. I'm no stranger to that goddam itch.' When she looked at him her eyes were fierce, as if for some reason her anger had shifted from Robin to him, but then her gaze softened. 'Ah, Bry, it's so easy to cave in and afterwards say I couldn't help it. And such a lie.'

Her hand, touching his cheek, lingered briefly.

He watched her go, confused. And then he decided he'd been given something, given it because she saw his need as great. Was it? As great as all that?

He slumped into the chair. He shut his eyes again, hoping his mind would drift aimlessly. Having been cued, however, it settled on the day of *in flagrante*.

In the great tradition, Bry had come home unexpectedly early. Afternoon classes had been cancelled due to an alleged bomb scare. (His department head, it was discovered subsequently, had over-reacted to a disgruntled parent's irate phone call.) Bry arrived at his door breathless, indescribably excited. Robin was there. Having pulled a hamstring in the finals of the Italian Open, she had been forced to default to Vera.

For her that meant an interruption to touring while she recovered. For Bry, however, it was a glittering prize. He hadn't hoped to set eyes on her until late in June, but here it was, only mid-May, and she was his exclusively for at least a week. Prize on top of prize: he was going to get to spend a bonus afternoon with her, thanks to Fred Hannay's most recent, heaven-sent act of paranoia.

He called her name as soon as he unlocked the door. She met him in the middle of the living-room, still tying the belt of a clinging black negligée. It was wonderfully transparent. At once his heart began hammering an erotic anvil chorus. She smiled, said something enrapturing, and lured him into the den where she converted him into an animal. During that interval her lover escaped unnoticed. A squad of jack-booted stormtroopers could have done the same.

Probably he would never have known, he always thought, if she had really intended him not to. It wouldn't have taken much to keep him out of the bedroom until she repaired the damage. Instead she allowed herself to slip into a post-coital doze, while Bry got up and collected discarded clothing. That woke her. Belatedly, she hurried after him. But when he saw the bed and made some unavoidable comment about its condition—it looked, after all, as if Agincourt had been fought there—she only sighed and kept silent.

How explain it, he'd wondered since. Did she crave the punishment she could so easily have evaded? Was that it? Perhaps. Or perhaps a million miles from that. It could have been, he'd thought, simply her way of getting free without having to frame the need in words. She hated quarrelling with him. He knew that. But he knew also that she was an enigma of a woman, mostly because she herself was so often ill-prepared for what she found herself doing.

The silence between them grew. During it his eyes remained fixed on the bed. He had no idea where her eyes were, possibly on her watch. Finally, having figured a few things out, he said, 'The business in the den was to cover a getaway?'

She frowned, lifted her hand, and stared at her fingers as if she had just gone one short. He pulled the hand down. 'Answer me.'

'It started that way.'

'I want you to say his name.'

It seemed to him there was a degree of tension in her smile, but that might have been wishful thinking, misery yearning for company. 'The name's not important,' she said.

'Not important? What is that supposed to mean? Do I take it then you're not in the grip of some overwhelming passion?'

Same smile. 'I *am* going to miss the way you talk.'

'You're leaving?'

'You're throwing me out. You just haven't got around to realizing it yet.'

He did realize it then, and it felt disorienting, hollowing. 'It was Boswell, wasn't it?' he said. 'I've seen the way he looks at you.'

'It wasn't Boz.'

'Then who was it?'

'Not important. You know it's not.'

'Damn you, don't *say* that to me. You're lying to protect him. I'll find him and beat the truth out of him.'

'Ah, Bry, he'd have you for breakfast,' she said gently.

And that was when he hit her. He had no idea he was going to, of course. It was as if some rogue force had broken loose. Open-handed but hard, the blow knocked her across the bed. She was on her feet instantly and back on the floor, knees slightly bent, staring at him, not in fear, but with a heightened alertness. He had surprised her. Competitor that she was, she was determined to be ready for whatever happened next. But blood trickled from the corner of her mouth where his class ring had cut her. He watched it, fascinated, hating it, hating himself for having caused it. He went to the window.

'It's nothing, a scratch.' Her voice was perfectly steady. He turned. She was at her vanity table mirror.

He kept silent.

After a moment she said, 'Now for God's sake listen to me. I don't want you mooning around and blaming yourself. This has nothing to do with you. It has to do with me and the stuff that's in me and the stuff that isn't. And I did warn you.'

'I'd better go now,' he said. 'I'll check into the Tri-Towns Hotel, and you can have tomorrow to do what you have to do around here. That's fair, isn't it? You don't have any interest in the apartment, do you? In keeping it, I mean.'

She shook her head.

'All right, then.'

As quickly as he could he got himself ready, but at the door he stopped. He didn't know why. If it was because he wanted to say something, he had no idea what that might be. Perhaps it was merely to prolong their connection for a few extra minutes, to stave off the alienation waiting for him on the other side of the door. He looked back into the room. She was standing there, hands tight at her sides, fists knotted, racked by a torment that, if incomprehensible to him, was certainly real enough. Without even hesitating, he crossed the room to her, took her in his arms, and actually made comforting sounds to her. Smoothing her hair, stroking her back. When he thought about all this later it made him writhe.

'I hit you,' he said. 'How could I have done a thing like that?'

'Don't,' she said harshly, pushing him away. 'You're such a damn fool.'

He ran until the hammer in his chest forced him to stop.

And where he wound up for the next two days was at the Horowitzes', being keened over and cosseted by Helen. But he remembered that only vaguely.

Jacob came in while they were still at coffee, filling the kitchen with his big frame and irrepressible gusto. Helen had predicted he'd be sky high, and he was, exuberant over a smashing success—the rapist-killer hadn't merely confessed, he had gushed.

Pinching Helen's cheek, touseling Bry's hair, bouncing out of his chair periodically like some odd species of dybbuk, oversized but essentially benign. 'Mirandized to a "t" and solid as a rock. We'll put the bastard away forever.' Repeating: 'Forever, forever.' Singing it out at the top of his lungs, his victory chant.

Later, over the chessboard, he was indomitable. Three games—a clean sweep, something he had never before managed. Chess, so much more than non-players think, a game of emotion.

Helen had gone to bed, so it was Jacob who walked Bry to the door. 'You going to her match Friday night?' he asked suddenly.

'Haven't decided.' He looked at Jacob. 'Should I?'

'Smart money's against it.'

'I can see how it would be.'

Jacob was silent a moment, rubbing his face hard. When he finished, gone was Jacob the Clown, replaced by the ever-lurking Jacob the Existentialist Funeral Director. 'Want to know what my old grampa used to say?'

Bry nodded.

'He used to say never belt a woman in the chops twice.'

'Really?'

'Uh-huh.'

'Do you know what your old grampa meant by that?'

'Sort of.'

In a way Bry did, too.

It was just after eleven when he left the Horowitz house, which was about a ten-minute walk from his own apartment. Half way there he got knocked down by a car. Not hurt, just barely clipped and tipped off balance, but shocked and frightened all the same.

The car didn't stop, and in the state he was in, it was hard to be sure of much. Still, he thought he knew who it was behind the wheel. He thought it was Jatie Ramirez, face set and angry.

A two and a four—those were the last digits of the licence plate. Bry stood in the middle of the road, waving his fist and screaming those numbers. Windows came open and a middle-aged woman in wrapper and curlers emerged from her house decently eager to help. But he hurried away from her.

He didn't get much sleep that night. He had a series of unsettling dreams. In the most lurid of them he found himself beating Tommy Boswell with a metal tennis racket until, bloodied and reeling, Boz turned into Robin, at which point Bry fled, pursued by Jatie Ramirez. He woke, sweating.

By the following morning, Bry had largely forgotten his dream. At breakfast, however, he unfolded the *Courier* and learned an attraction had been added to that night's card: a one-set exhibition between the rival coaches. Ramirez and Boswell would square off for a $5000 winner-take-all. In a photo awash with bonhomie, Vera hugged Jatie, and Robin embraced Tommy, all four beaming. Big, bright grins, so at odds with their dream expressions that sheer contrast evoked a re-run. It gripped unpleasantly. Dreams are only dreams, he told himself as he had told Robin yesterday, but minutes passed before he could shake off the effect.

He lifted the newspaper again. Yes? No? *Had* it been Jatie? And if it had been, did Jatie know it was Bry he had knocked down? Did he know it was anyone?

Other questions waited in the wings, but considered in daylight all seemed too melodramatic to be taken seriously. Jatie—Robin's warnings notwithstanding—had never given Bry the slightest cause for anxiety. They had met with reasonable frequency, and always Jatie had been cordial. Some other thin-faced, dark-bearded person had driven that car last night, Bry decided, tossing the paper aside.

The phone rang: Sherry, sounding enough like her sister to cause Bry his customary ten seconds of confusion.

'Robin asked me to call,' she said. 'She wants to make sure you'll be there tonight. She'd have called herself, but she figured I'd be harder to turn down.'

'You are.'

She laughed. There was something both rueful and

affectionate in that—as if they were fellow sufferers—and it brought her into sharper focus.

On certain days Sherry not only sounded like Robin, she looked like her, too. Those were days on which Robin wasn't around. When Robin was, Sherry could go very shadowy, dimming her colours as a chameleon might.

Sherry's fling on the tournament circuit had lasted little more than a year, a period during which she had never shown much more than average ability. In fact, her last professional match had been against Robin, a thirty-five-minute thumping. 'Baby Beats up on Little Sis,' one newspaper had unfeelingly reported.

After that she had accepted a post as Robin's manager-companion. She was smart and efficient, yet unobtrusive enough to be virtually unknown by her sister's adoring public. It occurred to him then that with Robin's bowing out Sherry's career was coming to a crossroads, too. He asked her about plans.

'Not sure of anything yet,' she said. 'I may just take it easy for a while. We'll see. I'm fixed all right for money so there's no hurry.' Her voice took on dryness. 'But wherever I go it won't be where Robin is.'

He tried to think of something neutral to say.

'Oh hell, I didn't mean that the way it sounded. It's just time for me to kick the habit, that's all. Bry, she really does desperately want you on scene.'

'All right, tell her she wins.'

A breath of relief. 'Thanks,' she said. 'That'll make life easier.'

A few seconds later she disconnected.

His last class finished at four, and as was his regimen these days he headed over to the Civic Center for his thirty-to forty-minute jogging session. The track, a quarter-miler, circled and overlooked the gym proper. There, on an *ad hoc* tennis court, Boswell and Ramirez were banging balls at each other, an exhibition in preparation for an exhibition. Around the railing a crowd of fifty or so was watching with interest. Bry joined.

Both coaches were tall men, but Jatie, though thinner, seemed also the stronger. He hit topspin forehands that looked ferocious, but which were interrupted by the net with noticeable frequency. Boz hit with less force and more accuracy. It was obvious that when they got down to business he'd have the edge, Bry thought, without much pleasure.

'Is that a Bryski I see before me?'

Vera Menchicov, in tennis costume, made her way towards him. Having drawn attention to herself, she became at once the centre of a clamour for autographs. She signed five, but then smilingly—a smile, however, that brooked no nonsense—she refused the sixth. She kissed him.

'Bryski, a sight for sore eyes.'

'And you as well.'

Their ritual greeting. From the day Robin had introduced them—ordering each to regard the other lovingly since they were her two favourite people in all the world—they had observed the form. For Bry's part it might well have gone deeper, except that she worried him. He always had the feeling she was hiding something complex and perhaps critical, at any rate something inimical to real friendship.

'Well, for damn sure she hides things,' Robin had said impatiently on the day he made this a point of discussion. 'If you were Vera wouldn't you be a hider?'

The answer was an unavoidable yes.

Vera's experience at hiding was extensive. A Russian Jew, she'd been born to politically active parents in whom the KGB had an on-going interest. Visits—usually nocturnal—had been unremitting. Interrogations—that included Vera, young as she was—were regularly scheduled. The dreaded fortress-prison Lubyanka loomed over them constantly, a staple of family life.

The week after Vera's fourth birthday long-term escape plans had come to fruition. In the dead of a September night, just before the snows, by freighter, by ferry, by haywagon, by flat-bed truck, and eventually by steamer, they fled to Canada and finally by air to the US.

No one, Bry acknowledged, could get past that kind of experience without being marked by it. Considered from this perspective, Vera, high spirited more often than not, was remarkable.

And whatever else she was, Vera was unquestionably a stunner: twenty-eight; dark hair, blue eyes; creamy, rose-tinted skin, and those high, built-to-last, Russian-princess cheekbones. Slender, tall—five-eleven in tennis shoes—she was both beautiful and imperious.

Her tennis game made a match. Picture-perfect strokes. And when she was right, a slashing, all-out aggressiveness that intimidated opponents into error. 'Charges the net like a damn Cossack,' Robin had once complained after being victimized. Vera the Great, they called her on those days when everything came together.

She stared down at the action below, patrician nose wrinkling, foot tapping, displeasure evident.

'And that's a teacher,' she said. 'If a student of his played that way Jatie would have his cojones. Or her . . . never mind, never mind.' She took Bry's arm. 'Come, get a cup of coffee with me. I want to talk to you.'

He allowed himself to be drawn along, but after a step or so she stopped to watch a drastically over-hit backhand. 'Jatie, Jatie, what's to become of you?' she said, half under her breath. She shook her head. 'Whose idea would you say this is? The exhibition, I mean. Guess.'

'Yours?'

'Absurd. Jatie's, of course.'

'Why of course?'

'Perhaps I'll tell you over coffee. Or perhaps I'll tell you something else. We'll see.' She glanced down. 'Boz will beat him tonight. He would not have last year, but last year was last year. Correct, my friend?'

'It always is.'

She smiled. 'Interesting how a clever man can make even

banality sound witty. Jatie is never witty, did you know that? Though once his muscles seemed to suffice.'

'When was that, last year?'

'Exactly. Now I find myself wishing he could be more like you. Does that surprise you, Bryski?'

'Have you said as much to him recently?'

'Of course not.'

But he was not convinced. The image of a looming car popped briefly into his mind before a tug on his arm moved him forward. She stopped again, however. 'Which one is your money on, Bryski?' Sly, calculated look. 'Dumb question. You would never bet on Boz.'

The coffee shop was a floor up from the gym. It was an odd hour, and the small, help-yourself premises—six-seat counter, ten tables pressed close—had only half a dozen other patrons. They got their coffee, found a table and sat down.

'Did I ever tell you the story of my life?' she asked.

'Bits here and there.'

'Do you want to hear it all?'

He thought about that and said, 'I wouldn't mind.'

'Damn if I don't believe you. That's a nice quality you have, Bryski. Baby always says so. I mean, you actually do listen to people. I never do. My guess is that's why she fell in love with you.'

'Because I listened to her?'

'That's right.'

'And when she fell out of love with me, was it because, just like that, I stopped listening to her?'

'No. It was because Baby falls out of love with people.' She grinned. 'Don't look now, please, but Jatie lurks on our outskirts. He wants to penetrate but won't unless I allow it. Should I? He is furious with me, you know. I told him last night I would not sleep with him any more, and so he is sulking. Not that he really wants to sleep with me that much, but he's gloomy about his prick these days. He thinks of it as on the endangered list. Steal a look now!'

He glanced across the room in time to see Jatie raise a

fist to pound the table he shared with Sherry. Though he finally brought it down without impact, effort had been required to achieve restraint. Bry saw him slump a little. He saw Sherry cover his hand with hers. Jatie seemed comforted.

'He'd be much better off with her,' Vera said. 'But he really wants me.'

'I thought he really wanted Robin.'

'Oh, everybody wants Baby, that's a given. But he knows down deep he can't have her. He thinks it's not quite the same with me. He thinks he can have me. He's wrong, but that's what he thinks. You've got that pinched look on your face, Bryski. It always tells me you're not computing. Tennis people are a confusing group to you.'

'True.'

'And yet we're such simple folk.'

'Are you?'

'Well, maybe not. Maybe we really are complex as hell, which is why we find ourselves so endlessly interesting. That follows, does it not, Bryski?'

He could not help smiling.

She smiled, too. 'Behold the Narcissi. Is that an acceptable plural?'

'It'll do.'

Her eyes narrowed. 'And you, too, would do better with Sherry, but the truth is your prick isn't any smarter than the common run. Explain why all men want exactly what they can't have.'

'Just men?'

'I stand corrected,' she said. 'Wanting at cross purposes. Is that the human condition, Bryski?'

'I don't know.'

She raised a brow in mock astonishment. 'But you must. You have to. You are the professor. I mean, the whole tour knows that's what you are. Whenever anybody needs an answer Baby invariably says—wait, I'll ask the professor bird. That's the locker-room joke. Oh, come now, Bryski. I didn't mean *you* were. *It* is.'

All right.'

Her face clouded. 'Past tense. Baby *used* to say. So hard, so hard to believe. Wimbledon—and no Baby Robin Cantrell. US Open—no Baby Robin. I know there's supposed to be life after Baby, but what can it be like? I've played her ever since I was a pigtailed junior, thirteen years old. Forty-seven times in all. I've known her longer than anyone except my parents. I've laughed with her, fought with her, got high with her, cried in her arms. How is one to manage a world without Baby in it?'

'Adjustments are possible,' he said.

Her glance softened. 'Sorry, I forgot you're a fellow traveller.'

He drained his coffee.

'Another?'

He shook his head.

'So what did you think of them?' she asked.

'Of what?'

She peered at him. 'Damn you, Bryski. Are you, or are you not having me on?'

'I haven't the least notion what you're talking about.'

For a moment her scepticism seemed proof against this, but then she said, 'OK, let's take you at face value. Baby didn't mention threats?'

'What kind of threats?'

'She didn't show them to you?'

'Are you saying she's been receiving hate mail?'

'Two notes. One last week, one the week before. Well, not threats exactly, but bad stuff. Words cut from newspapers and glued on, you know? The first one simply said, *Remember May 10th*. The second: *A lying bitch deserves no pity*. Exact quotes.' She was silent a moment. 'Bryski?'

He stared at her but said nothing.

'May 10th,' she said, a hint of apology in her voice.

'I heard you.'

May 10th of course was the day of infamy. Or, from Robin's perspective, liberation day.

'No, Bryski, don't be angry with your Vera. I don't really think it was you. Not your style.'

'Did she show the notes to Boswell?'

'Not his style either.'

'Whose, then?'

She grinned. 'Could be Vera's.'

'Did Robin show the notes to anyone else?'

'For instance?'

'I don't know—the police?'

'I doubt it.'

'Why not?'

'I didn't ask her, but if I had to guess I would say it was because she was reluctant to make them that important. Do you understand, Bryski? She wanted them to be the result of some stupid but harmless prank. No worse than that. Showing them to the police . . . then she'd have to take them seriously. God, remember that time in Boston last year when that madman came charging out of the Copley Plaza waving a bolo knife?' She smacked her forehead. 'Of course you do. You're the one who stuck your foot out and tripped him. If it hadn't been for you . . . Anyway, that's what she's afraid of, you see. Or something worse.'

'Worse?'

'Someone she knows would make it worse.'

'Someone like me in other words. Is that why she came to the apartment yesterday? To confront me with them.'

'Confront? Not you, Bryski. You're one of the few people in this world Baby shies from confronting. She'd have to be boiling mad. Or stoned. But yes, she said she was going to show them to you.'

'I wonder why she didn't. Or even mention them.'

'What did she do?'

His glance slid away from hers, lured by a dried twig snagged on his sneaker lace. He kicked at it with his other foot.

'Oh God,' she said. 'The little trollop tried to haul you into bed.'

He had not intended to respond, but Jatie, pounding his back, removed that option anyway. Ostensibly, the blows were in good fellowship. The heaviness of them, however, suggested a sub-text.

'*Serious.* Such serious talk here. What's being cooked up? Some hot new deal? *El Profesor* is about to steal another señorita from me?'

'He can't steal what you don't own,' Vera said sharply, but then shifted to make room for him and for Sherry, too.

'Sorry,' Sherry said with an apologetic glance to signal she was under duress.

'For what? for trying to keep a fool from behaving like one?'

Jatie's dark eyes went hard, but he rested them on Vera for only an instant before swinging his glance towards Bry. He had one of those long, narrow, hawk-nosed faces that went well with melancholy or war. Or both, as in a Velasquez Bry had seen once, a painting of a weary, blood-drenched conquistador. The thick black beard surrounded cherry lips and came to a point. Like some kind of weapon, he aimed it at Bry.

'Both ways, *Profesor*. That is how one should learn to look before crossing the street. Did they not teach you this as a child?'

Bry kept silent.

'What is the man talking about?' Vera demanded.

'Tell her,' Jatie said. 'You have my permission.'

Bry shrugged. 'Someone almost ran me down last night. Until now I wasn't sure who it was.'

Vera stared at Jatie. 'Were you drunk?'

He smiled. 'Sober I would not have missed him.'

'Oh, you idiot. You murderous . . . Why don't you go back to Argentina before you do kill someone? Or someone kills you.'

Her exit was magnificent though unobserved. Clearly none was eager to risk attracting her attention.

But for Jatie, Vera's departure pulled a plug. Ferocity

drained from him. 'She is right,' he said. 'She is always right. I am a fool.'

'Jatie, leave off,' Sherry said. 'Go on back to the hotel and get some rest. You've got a match tonight.'

He lifted Vera's cup and examined it unseeingly. 'We were playing cards, Boswell and I, as we have done fifty, a hundred times before. Out of nowhere, there is Vera. She stands behind him instead of me. She puts her hand on *his* shoulder, studying *his* cards. Well, does that mean anything? Of course not. I know it now, knew it then. But in an instant this fool Ramirez—' a blow to his chest for emphasis—'is issuing challenges. Five thousand dollars. Mother of God, it has been a while since I had money like that to throw away.' He put the cup down and turned to Bry. 'Tell me why I do things I cannot explain. Why am I full of such rage?'

Bry thought his safest course was to treat the questions as rhetorical, but Jatie grabbed a handful of his shirt and pulled on it. A cup fell off the table, shattered. Patrons' breaths were audible. The coffee shop's proprietor began swabbing the counter top with furious energy. Back and forth went his rag. And so did Bry go back and forth while Jatie, using the shirt as leverage, alternately pulled and pushed.

'Tell me,' Jatie said.

Sherry pounded his knuckles with her coffee spoon. 'Enough,' she said. 'Or I swear I'll start beating on your head.'

Jatie freed him but kept his eyes fixed, except now they were no longer savage. They implored. 'Take pity, *Profesor.*'

'Tell you what?' Bry said. 'What is there to tell you? That life can drive a man crazy? All right, it can.'

Jatie sighed heavily. A moment later he rose abruptly from his chair, knocking it off balance and having to clutch at it to keep it from falling. He left, shaking his head, life as incomprehensible to him as before Bry spoke.

'That damn woman,' Sherry said. 'She's torturing him. She thinks she's tired of him, but she isn't quite sure. So while she makes up her mind she keeps him in hell. I hate a woman who'll do that.'

'He has my sympathy,' Bry said.

Her eyes flickered, and he was certain her mind had followed his, from Jatie's case to his own, but when she spoke it was still of Jatie.

'There are sides to him,' she said. 'He can be such an oaf, and he can also be—lovely. When he was Robin's teacher he took me on, though he didn't have to. He wasn't being paid for it. But you see he's basically a sweet-natured man, honestly he is, when he's feeling himself. Anyway, he saw how needy I was—adolescent needy, do you understand?'

'Yes.'

She pursed her lips. 'Did he really knock you down?'

'I think what happened is I got my feet tangled and tripped.'

'Did you report it?'

'No. As I say, I'm not at all sure he really went after me.'

'But even if he only meant to scare you. He—God, he's never done anything like that before that I know of.' She began to shiver. She hugged herself.

'What's wrong?'

'Nothing.' But she wouldn't look at him. She shuddered again, more deeply, and said, 'This is ridiculous.'

'Are you cold?'

'No, that's not it. It's just—God, I feel stupid.'

'You're never that,' he said, and to his surprise made her angry.

'How would you know? You think you really know anything about me? Well, you don't. You've got this idea about me. Don't deny it, I know it's true. Safe, sane, and dull as dishwater. But the fact is I can be as crazy as my sister any day in the week. I mean that.'

'All right.'

'Damn it, it's true. I once almost killed Robin. No way you believe that, right? Well, it happened. I was sixteen and tried to push her out a window. Ask Robin. Ask Aunt

Win.' Once more her shoulders shook, but since this paroxysm was milder and briefer than the others he decided to ignore it.

'Why?' he asked after a moment. 'I mean, what had she done?'

'I don't even remember that now. A dumb quarrel about a skirt, I suppose. Or a sweater. All I remember is how crazy I was. Damn, why am I telling you this? You won't want anything to do with me. You'll despise me.'

'That's not possible,' he said.

The response was both quicker and more ardent than he himself had expected—so much so that he felt as if some internal coup had been mounted, a kind of palace revolution as the result of which long suppressed emotions had been freed. But this made him uneasy. He was aware that his palms were sweating. He took a deep breath, however, and then another, and then suddenly understood that what he had experienced was one of those watershed moments when words pop out uncensored, and the speaker hearing them realizes he's tapped into his own core. An insight, in short. Meaning what? Simply that she was more important to him than he'd ever taken the time to consider.

Her hands were folded in her lap, clasped hard. 'I can tell you now what the shivering and shuddering was all about. Do you want me to?'

'Please.'

'It's not all that complicated really. It was shock. Just like that, I had this vivid picture of you being hit, being hurt. Badly, I mean.'

'I see.'

'Do you?'

He had to clear his throat and even then the words managed to get stuck half way. 'Yes,' he said. 'I think I do.'

She seemed to relax a little, as if his illness at ease had had the effect of lessening hers. 'In for a penny, in for a pound,' she said. 'Are you and Robin patching it up?'

'No.'

'Sure?'

'It's not going to happen,' he said grimly.

'That sounds as if Robin has been pestering. Has she been?'

He didn't answer.

Her eyes, a darker blue than Robin's, lit with anger. 'Give her the pretty bauble, and she's bored in nothing flat. Take it away, and all hell breaks loose. Sorry. You probably think that's—'

'Understated,' he said.

'Really?'

'Of course.'

'But you never complain.'

'Complain? To whom? Who's the god in charge of fixing things like that?'

She sighed. 'I think he's gone out of business.'

After a moment she said, 'And yet I love and am grateful to Robin. I owe her. But that doesn't mean I'm blind to her faults. Nor is she to mine, for that matter. We fight, you know. We've fought about you once or twice. Did she tell you?'

'No.'

She lifted her hands from her lap and placed them on the table, palms up, seeming to study them as if the curve of a lifeline were the issue. But he guessed she was buying time. Or perhaps hoping for something to happen that would take the next few minutes out of her control. Nothing did.

'Bry, should I shut up? I can do that and survive. I swear that's true.'

'Of course it is.'

'But I like you. Probably, I—' She bit her lip as if to make herself stop, and when she continued the words came a shade more carefully. 'Probably I like you a lot and have from the moment Robin brought you around, which is no doubt what we fought about, though neither of us ever exactly admitted it. Anyway, I think you like me, too.'

'I do.'

'Are you interested in finding out how much?'

They didn't hear Robin until she tossed a pair of rackets

on to one of the empty chairs and commandeered the other.

She wore a loose grey sweatshirt over green warm-up pants, and it was clear she had just come off the court. Despite the perspiration still beading on her forehead, she looked lovely. But as she tipped her chair against the wall and studied dark red fingernails raptly she did not look happy.

'How old am I, Sherry? Am I eighty? That's how I moved today, elephant feet.'

'You always have a rotten practice just before a match,' Sherry said. 'The worse the practice, the better you play.'

'And you always tell me that, and all it is is bullshit.'

After that, as if by mutual consent, they settled into becoming a three-figure sculpture garden. Minutes passed; none of them spoke. They just sat there in a strange, sullen silence until one of the statues suddenly jerked into life.

'Stuff to do,' Sherry said and left abruptly.

Bry might have followed her. It was in his mind to do so, but then Robin said, 'I feel like I'm unravelling.' And though he sat back he was careless enough to be caught focusing on the departing sister.

'Was I breaking something up?' A glint came into her eyes. 'I was, wasn't I?'

'Unravelling how?'

But the glint was brighter now. Malice had energized her, and she straightened. 'You like being a hand-me-down, Bry?'

He rose, but she grasped his wrist, hanging on to him. 'Wrong, wrong,' she said and with her free hand used an invisible eraser on a nonexistent blackboard. 'Definitely wrong. Forgive? Please?'

He allowed her to pull him back down.

'I think I'm scared,' she said.

'Of what?' he asked cautiously.

'I . . . don't know. Well, I do know. That is, I think I know, but I don't think I can explain it.'

'Vera told me about the threats.'

'Oh, those. I figured out who sent those.'

'Who?'

But she shook her head impatiently. 'That's just silliness.'

'Silliness?'

'That's all they are.' She was still holding his wrist and dug her nails into it now, hurting. 'How about if you let me come home?'

'No.'

'I'll be good, I swear I will. And I'll love you just to death. Wait'll you see.'

'No.'

She leaned forward. Her eyes seemed to have darkened to purple or cobalt blue or one of those other unfathomable shades. 'Anyone but Sherry,' she said.

'I don't know what you're talking about.'

'You've got this vengeful side to you, Bry. You won't admit it, but you have. And I don't want you *using* Sherry. She's fragile. She may not look it, but she is. And she's never, ever had anyone. She's like that poet, that Emily Dickinson you're so crazy about. She could crack . . . crack wide open . . . if she was to get the wrong—'

'That's absurd. That's such nonsense even you can't take it seriously.'

'Can't I?'

Once more he got up to go, and once more she stopped him. 'No, no, I can't. Of course I can't. What it is is a sister thing. You don't have any idea what that means, but it's the way sisters are, and I just couldn't bear to be left for her.'

'Left for her,' he said bitterly.

'Yes. For her, for her. You'd let me come home if it weren't for her. Maybe you don't even know you would, but you would.'

The idea intrigued her. He watched its appeal grow, thinking, as he had often before, that the poltergeist in her lay so close to her surface you could see it mottling her skin.

And now would come variations on a theme, he knew.

'She's just making trouble, of course. Little Miss Butter-Wouldn't-Melt. Revenge, that's what it is. Little Miss

Second-Fiddle her whole life, and finally here's a chance to get back at me. Jealousy, that's all it is. And I'll tell her so to her face. You think I won't? Well, I will. Tonight. Just watch me.'

Anger wanted to explode, but for once he was able to master it, biting off words. His face was on fire. Conscious of having attracted spectator interest, he forced himself down to his chair.

'Have it your way,' he said.

She lifted her hands for further fingernail study and muttered something deprecating about their scarlet disguise. She tipped herself back against the wall.

'I'm going to leave now,' he said.

'Sure,' she said. 'Whenever I want to fight you want to leave. Damn you, Bry. Don't you know what that does to a person?'

But her voice was softer, and her smile had apology lurking in it. And then, in the next instant, the smile was transformed, blazing up the way it did when she was feeling pressure on the court—the key element in a competitor's mask. Having recognized it for what it was, Bry turned as Hattie Lockridge entered the coffee shop.

Tom Boswell trailed her.

If Hattie was aware of Robin's presence, she pretended not to be. She picked up a menu and went invisible behind it, while Boswell shifted his chair, blocking the sight of Robin and Bry together as if it were offensive to him.

In only her second year on the tour, Hattie Lockridge was already recognized as one of the specials. Red flag phrases were being dusted off for her: 'tremendously talented', 'unlimited potential'. 'The Lock', they called her, in reference not only to her name, but to the dogged way she stayed in a point no matter how hot the day or how long the rally.

But there was a minority view.

'No flash, no dash,' Bry had heard Vera say. 'A lumpy-dump who thinks laughing makes your teeth fall out.'

Hattie was short and stocky with the thick shoulders and

arms central to her smash-'em-up power game. She had mouse-like hair and a round, freckled, solemn face. Her eyes were extraordinary, though. They were pale blue and looked older than the rest of her.

As Bry glanced towards her he saw her lower the menu, stare at Robin, and mouth the word, 'Asshole.'

Robin rose at once to cross the room. Reflexively, Bry grabbed for her, caught her shoulder, slowing her, until she whirled and shook him off hard. He lost his balance, falling over the same chair that had figured in Jatie's exit.

'Bry,' Robin said, kneeling to help him up. 'I'm sorry.' And then (not really meaning to, he acknowledged later) she began to giggle. 'Oh, Bry, was anyone ever clumsier than you? I mean, if there's one chair in the middle of a fucking desert...'

He rolled away from her outstretched hands. Attempting to rise too quickly, he slipped and went down again. Finally, he got himself erect and moments later into a desperate, lurching exit.

'Bry, come back here, damn it. Oh, for God's sake, someone stop him.'

Faces pivoted towards him as he hurled by. Among them, he was conscious of Boswell's. It seemed for an instant that in response to his mistress's bidding Boswell's aim was to block the door. Bry would have choked him if he'd tried.

It took Bry the better part of two hours that evening to descend from fury to a state of rueful self-awareness. A pair of stiff martinis helped. By seven, however, he had even generated laughter once or twice at his own absurdity.

He was just finishing dinner, and, over coffee, beginning to replay the conversation with Sherry—in the hope of inching up on its meaning—when the phone rang. It was Fred Hannay, head of Bry's department, and party of the second part to a mutual detestation that had begun on sight.

Hannay was a small, wiry man, a good five inches shorter than Bry's five-nine. Minutes after his first arrival on campus he and Bry had shared the incident that set the tone for their relationship.

Backing out of a doorway, encumbered with books and other pedagogic paraphernalia, Bry had bumped into Hannay. 'Didn't see you there,' Bry said, intending nothing more than a simple apology. What had registered with Hannay was that he would have been seen had there been more of him.

He was affronted. It was vivid in his face. Later in the day, Bry was officially introduced. The conversation between them then was brief. But memorable, Bry thought later.

'You have a reputation,' Hannay said, 'for going your own way.'

'Do I?'

'Oh, indeed. I suppose you call that integrity or some such.'

Diplomatic responses occurred to Bry, but at that moment they seemed particularly unattractive, and he said, 'What would you call it, sir?'

Hannay nodded, and nodded again as if some private theory had been vindicated. 'I don't like you, Gilchrist. Gil*christ*,' he said, lengthening the 'i' in the second syllable of Bry's name. 'I suspect that's who you think you are, some sort of Christ figure. What do I call it? If I have to call it insubordination, sir, I warn you I will not tolerate it.'

Their glances met and locked, and though Hannay's was the first to fall away Bry was not reassured by a sense of victory. He knew he had made an enemy and that the enemy was implacable. He considered himself fortunate to be already tenured.

Still, things might have improved if the two hadn't so clearly cherished their antipathy. Occasionally, Bry experienced second thoughts about this on the grounds that it was childish, but the fact was, he enjoyed being Hannay's gadfly. He knew he stuck in Hannay's craw, and savoured the discomfort this caused. In a sense it defined him, he sometimes thought. Despising Hannay for his narrow-mindedness, his pretensions, his ambition, raised Bry in his own estimation, and since Hannay was never going to let him off the hook anyway, he had early on decided not to wriggle.

'Have I pulled you away from your dinner, Bry? Sorry if I have.'

Hannay had one of those deep, commanding voices, which he capped with a trace of Oxbridge. You could tell he admired his voice, and it *was* formidable.

'That's all right.'

'I'm afraid we have rather an emergency on our hands.' He didn't sound afraid, Bry thought. He sounded eager.

But suddenly Bry knew who the emergency involved. Her name was Norma Braun, a student in his graduate seminar on the early American realists—a loner, resistant so far to every attempt to draw her into the group. Her written work was excellent, but steadily, it seemed to him, she grew more remote, more ephemeral, like some kind of delicate plant, waning towards the end of its season.

She was a tall, thin girl with cropped hair and a needle-sharp nose, invariably reddened by allergy or cold. But she had nice brown eyes, and he liked her.

He had tried talking to her. Was she worried about something, something he might be able to help her with? If so, she wouldn't say, her pale skin going dead white as she shuffled feet desperate to carry her from the room.

She had eleven fellow seminarians, a particularly lively collection. They, too, had made attempts to break down the walls. After several unrewarding failures, however, they had given up and now acted as if she didn't exist: eleven Mark Twains and an Alice James fading away neurasthenically.

It both exasperated and worried Bry, but he hadn't been able to figure out what to do about it. In that first moment he was actually glad Hannay had become aware of the situation. Another view, even Hannay's, might be useful, he told himself.

'Norma Braun,' he said on cue.

'How—'

'I just had a hunch.' And then, chillingly, he had another. But he couldn't get himself to put that one into words. 'Sorry, Fred. Suppose I just let you say what you called to say.'

'I rather think that might be a good idea.' Hannay cleared his throat. 'Norma Braun is recovering from a sleeping pill overdose.'

'Oh God.'

'Recovering, Bry, *recovering*. There's no need to—'

'Where is she, Tri-Towns General?'

'That is correct. The Provost called me, and now I'm calling you. Are you perhaps wondering why with such despatch?'

Until that moment, he hadn't been.

'It seems she left you a note. I went by your office with some scheduling changes and found it there, slipped under your door. Thinking it might be important, I picked it up, of course.'

'Of course,' Bry said blandly.

There was a moment of silence, during which he sensed in Hannay a strong inclination to expound on the matter of a department head's prerogatives, but Hannay had other fish to fry. 'I have the note here with me.'

'What does it say?'

'My dear Bryant, how can I possibly know? I wonder if I might see you in my rooms.'

'Now?'

'Well, the tower clock struck seven a few minutes back. Within the hour?'

'Suppose I just dash over to the hospital first—'

'That's hardly necessary. I've been assured she's resting comfortably. On the other hand, we do have matters of some importance before us, and those should be addressed promptly.'

'Such as?'

'The note.'

'I'm not sure I follow.'

Hannay cleared his throat again, and as if that were not sufficient to heighten the moment, paused lengthily.

'Bry, I'm in no way accusing you of anything, but you can see, I'm sure, that it's my responsibility to investigate fully. A young female student has attempted suicide, or at least it seems she has. Is this the result of some dereliction on . . . our part?'

'You mean my part?'

'Well, perhaps I do.'

'Then perhaps you'd best say exactly what's on your mind.'

'Yes. I agree. Pussy-footing in cases like this serves no useful purpose.'

'In cases like this,' Bry said softly.

Hannay was undeterred. 'In cases like this a department head is obliged to ask himself—am I confronted with the result of an improper relationship between a young girl entrusted to my care and one of my staff? This sealed note could quite possibly be an indicator.'

'You want me to come over and open it?'

'In my presence, yes. I very much think I'll have to ask you to drop everything else.'

'How did you get hold of the note?'

'How?'

'My office door is locked after hours. You've had a key made?'

He said nothing.

'Fred . . . ?'

The big voice boomed out like a shell-burst. 'I must say, Bry, I'm beginning to find your attitude obstructive. It's seven-ten now. I'll expect you at half past.'

'Open the damn thing yourself,' Bry said and hung up.

Grabbing his coat, he hurried out the door, focused on Norma and the hospital exclusively. Which meant, of course, that he completely forgot about Robin's match. And nothing else in his life was to cost him so much.

HELEN AND JACOB
IN LOVE AND WAR

CHAPTER 1

Mrs Brent, small and bustling, aimed her friendly smile at Helen and said regretfully, 'Maybe you'd better not wait.'
'Is that what he told you to tell me?'
'No. He didn't tell me anything. He just . . .'
'I'll wait.'
'Oh, he can be so—' But then she broke off, glancing guiltily behind her as if the man whose office she guarded had capabilities that included the extrasensory. She scurried to her desk. Her PC went back into action.
Helen wandered over to the wall to gaze at pictures, one of which showed Hannay about to crush an overhead. He looked pretty good, like the very decent club player he was reputed to be.
In all the other photos he was with companions so blatantly self-aware you just knew they were important. Helen recognized some of them. One of them was the university president. Another their mayor.
'Why can't people treat—' But again Mrs Brent put a stop to herself, this time biting her lip. 'I'm sorry.'
'Hey,' Helen said, 'waiting is something I'm terrific at. I may be the world's champ.' Settling into a handsome, though not very comfortable, chair to begin the besieging.
'You're sure you wouldn't like a coffee? It'd be no trouble. Honestly.'
Helen shook her head. She then shut her eyes to indicate she was pleasantly occupied and no longer to be worried about. For a moment Mrs Brent's warm, animated expression remained printed inside her lids. Then, perhaps by force of contrast, another face replaced it; a still one, blue-lipped, grey, cold as marble to the touch. Helen shuddered. Annoyed, she told herself to get real, get professional.
To speed the process she conjured up cranky, old Hank Carlucci, the evidence technician who, despite the

uncertainty of his moods, had been the police academy's best in crime scene investigation. He hadn't just taught. He'd dared his students not to learn:

'Traces.' Spitting the word at them as if they were Capulets *en masse* to his Montague. 'Some of this, some of that. That's the central premise of crime scene investigation—that the perp is going to leave you a message. Maybe he's going to take a piss and without thinking lift the toilet seat. Maybe he's going to light a cigarette and drop a matchbook with a big fat thumbprint on it. Perps ain't rocket scientists, they're assholes. And what assholes do is they leave you little love notes. So all you got to do is keep your stupid eyes open and look for them.'

Helen had always been drawn to that notion that, despite themselves, perps sent messages. That these could be decoded, provided you were good enough at the game. And that if your bent was optimistic you could infer from this a quality in the nature of evil that hungered for punishment.

Still, on that awful night two weeks ago, having gone along on the call over Jacob's protests, she had stood next to him, heart hammering. The naked, maltreated body they stared down at had sent no gamesman's messages. Instead the messages had been of an abstract kind, metaphysical messages of loss, of waste, of fear, and of mortality.

Her fingers had tightened on Jacob's bicep. Turning to her, he had said bleakly, 'Sometimes I think people are a shitty idea.'

But in a way all that had been before the fact.

Suddenly the case had become hers.

As ever, for Helen, that category of fact changed everything...

Professor Hannay was perfect, Helen thought, taking a seat opposite him twenty minutes later. Perfectly tweeded, perfectly shod, perfectly coiffed, perfectly cologned. Everything in his perfectly smooth face was in perfect proportion to everything else. His thin black moustache was perfectly trimmed. His handsome desk was perfectly fashioned from solid black walnut. His Arabian carpet was a perfect Bokhara. His Piranesi prints were perfectly chosen, his pipes perfectly aligned in their driftwood rack, his view a pleasing prospect of picture-perfect quad.

But he was short, and he hated that, she guessed. She was glad he did. Her aversion to him had been as instinctive as Bry's.

Hannay's glance at his discreetly expensive gold watch was accompanied by a sigh, Helen's cue to begin unfolding whatever frivolous and time-wasting tale had brought her to his office.

'I'm a private investigator hired by Bryant Gilchrist,' she said, withdrawing her notebook from her purse but holding it closed on her lap.

'So my secretary informs me,' he said. 'She also informs me you threatened to take up residence in my outer office unless I agreed to see you.'

'Promised,' she said mildly.

'Pardon?'

'Promised, not threatened.'

'Yes. Well, now that you've forced your way in, what is it you hope to gain?'

'A little help.'

'Am I to take it, then, that Bryant has been apprehended?'

'Apprehended?'

'The police are looking for him, aren't they?'

'They'd like to talk to him, yes, but he hasn't been charged with a crime.'

'As yet,' he said.

Helen kept silent.

He stared at her as if he expected the impact of slate grey eyes to be daunting, but it was not. Helen had been stared at before.

'I'm not sure I understand,' he said. 'If Bry is still among the missing how has he managed to hire you?'

'By phone. Last night.'

'Ah, another of those mysterious calls from nowhere.'

Helen didn't smile. 'Why mysterious? He called to hire me. No, he didn't say where he is, but he has his reasons for choosing not to. Though I may not agree with them, they don't strike me as mysterious. His previous phone calls weren't very mysterious either. Their purpose was to tell the police what he felt they'd want to know.'

'Oh, were they?'

'Yes.'

'I trust the police were as unimpressed as I was. As even the reporter was, who wrote the story for the *Courier*. One needed very little skill to read between *those* lines. As unimpressed, in fact, as the universe was and is.' He leaned forward aggressively. 'Minus those on his payroll.'

'The universe gets it wrong from time to time,' she said. 'It happens.'

Tongue against teeth produced an abrupt, impatient noise. 'Mrs Horowitz, you've made a useless trip. I regard Bryant Gilchrist as an unfortunate young man, but beyond that I simply do not have the luxury of giving much thought to him right now. I have a department to run. His . . . behaviour has complicated my life enormously.'

'Has it?'

'Of course it has. For one thing, I need a replacement. Until I find one . . . well, never mind, never mind. That has nothing to do with you, does it?' He looked at his watch again.

'What behaviour specifically?' Helen asked.

'Oh, please.'

'Do you mean his behaviour two weeks ago Friday night, or his behaviour in general?'

For answer he raised his eyes ceilingward as if seeking there the intervention of some *deus ex machina*. Helen waited. He said nothing. The game of silence continued until she allowed him to win.

'Concerning that Friday night,' she said, 'Bry claims to have spent a good part of it with Norma Braun.'

'So I understand. What a pity she can't corroborate.'

'He says he arrived at Tri-Towns General around half past seven, found a—'

'Mrs Horowitz, I must ask you to cease and desist. I'm not the least bit interested in what Bry Gilchrist did or didn't do that Friday night. Or any other night for that matter. That being the case, there is no real point in prolonging this interview, is there?'

'I guess I don't see it that way.'

Irritation pursed his lips. 'Perhaps you are bent on forcing me to call the police,' he said.

'You could call them,' she said. 'But after they bounce me I'll come back. And I'll keep coming back until I get done what I'm here to do. On the other hand, I'm asking for fifteen minutes, no more. Why jerk my chain?'

He took three breaths, calculatedly deep, while shutting his eyes and permitting his arms to dangle, a process she identified as stress management. It seemed to work. In a moment he was gazing at her as equably as if lost temper had not been an issue. Moreover, she sensed she had earned something from him—grudging respect, the kind bullies give when they realize they're going to have to shift ploys.

'You are a singularly obstinate woman,' he said thoughtfully.

'I've been told that.'

He got up, went to his window, and adjusted the blind. The sunlight had enough substance to dapple the carpet prettily. He stood there a moment staring out at his picturesque quad and showing off his profile. Well-shaped nose, firm chin, it was a nearly perfect profile.

'Fifteen minutes. Not a second longer,' he said in his nearly perfect basso.

'Thank you.' She consulted her notebook. 'Bry arrived at the hospital at approximately seven-thirty, found a parking space a block or so away. But as he approached the front steps he saw Norma Braun descending at a run. He caught up to her. She was distraught, he says.

'After persuading her to sit in his car, he managed to calm her. It wasn't easy. She cried off and on for almost an hour. She then said she wanted to return to her room, and he offered to accompany her. He wanted to stay with her. It bothered him that he'd been unable to get her to say anything about her emotional state, except that it was beyond his understanding, beyond anybody's.

'She refused his offer, and when he persisted he saw that she was becoming angry. She accused him of not trusting her, so he backed off. She promised to get right into bed. Reluctantly, he let her go, and that was the last he saw of her.' Helen looked up. 'According to the medical examiner's report, it was somewhere between ten and eleven that she jumped to her death, in other words within an hour after she left him. Her body wasn't discovered until one a.m., by a security guard, but you probably read that in the *Courier*.'

Somewhere a clock was ticking. A stomach rumbled, hers she thought detachedly.

'A tragedy,' he said.

'Do you blame Bry for it?'

Resuming his seat, he lifted a small, perfectly carved pipe from the rack and fondled it lovingly. 'Once owned by Douglas MacArthur,' he said. 'I have a letter attesting to how sweet-smoking it is.' He smiled. 'Filthy habit, don't you think?'

She waited.

He put the pipe back. 'No, I do not blame Bry,' he said. 'In Judge Hannay's *ex-officio* but not inconsequential Court of Pure and Practical Justice, Bry stands acquitted. Not guilty, say I. Are you surprised?'

'Yes,' Helen admitted.

The gleam of perfect teeth underscored his pleasure.

'Actually, it makes me wonder if maybe you've got a piece of evidence I'd very much like a look at,' she said.

'What on earth could that be?'

'Maybe she wrote something?'

'To me?'

'To . . . someone.'

'Well, certainly not to me. My dear Mrs Horowitz, I exchanged good-days with her twice or thrice a semester, but no confidences, I assure you. I share only in what is now common knowledge, which is, of course, that this was Miss Braun's third attempt to do away with herself and that she had been subject to bouts of melancholia ever since the shocking automobile accident that took the lives of her parents and younger sister as they were on their way here to see her. Two years ago, I believe. But heavens, none of that is Bry's fault. Poor Bry has enough on his plate without that.'

Helen studied him for a moment.

His expression remained placid.

She returned to her notes. 'Bry says he was back in his car shortly after nine. By then it had begun raining fairly heavily. On the way home the car skidded on wet leaves, went up on the sidewalk at Frazier and Poplar and hit that high kerb in front of the American Legion ball field. Flat tyre. It was almost eleven before he got it changed.'

'And I suppose no one witnessed any of that.'

'No one he knows of.'

'Ah, too bad.'

'Professor Hannay, I tell you this in detail because it all seems entirely plausible to me. I had hoped it might seem the same to you.'

'Why?'

On the point of batting that back to him hard, she held fire. Instead she said, 'I gather you and Bry have a history.'

'A history?'

'People in your department say you rubbed each other the wrong way.'

He smiled. 'I'll be blunt. In my view he is—was—an obstacle. He stands—stood—in the way of department progress. I have serious ambitions for my small realm, Mrs Horowitz. Ambitions, may I add, that I share with both the Provost and President Collier. We want our faculty, all our faculty, on the cutting edge.' He paused, built a steeple from his fingers and studied her over its top. Then he shut his eyes. When he opened them they gleamed with battle light. 'Bryant Gilchrist thought tenure rendered him invulnerable. He was wrong. Had he not done for himself, I would have found a way to do for him. How's that for a moment of candour?'

'I appreciate it, sir.'

He nodded. 'Now that you do, let me assure you it never took place. The ultra-loyal Mrs Brent, my secretary, will swear she was in the room every second you were and that we spoke only inconsequentials. Unlike Bry, Mrs Brent is sharply aware of who makes a bad enemy. Do we understand each other?'

'Yes.'

'Good. In addition, may I inform you that what seems so plausible to you strikes me as absolute hogwash. Almost four hours during which he was as unseen as if he were Mr Wells's Invisible Man ... hogwash, I say. And it must have seemed so to him, or why did he run?'

'He might not have if things had worked out a little better. He drove to our house. I wish we'd been there, but we weren't. He sat in his car waiting for us ... about half an hour or so, he said. He turned on the radio. When he learned the police were already looking for him, he panicked.'

'An innocent person does not panic, Mrs Horowitz.'

'Are you so sure?'

'Aren't you?'

'I've seen every sort of person panic. What's panic, Professor Hannay? It's being too scared to think straight. That's never happened to you?'

'No, dear lady, and I very much doubt it's happened to you, either.'

'It has,' she said simply.

But she could see he didn't believe her. It was obvious that he viewed panic as something forever subject to self-control. Moreover, she thought, in his case it might be. She found herself wondering if he could love anyone, doubting it. Love implied the willingness to trust. She wondered how old he'd been the last time he'd done that, and the answer she supplied at once made her feel sorry for him.

Only briefly. You didn't feel lastingly sorry for the hangman, and it had occurred to her that in Judge Hannay's Court of Pure and Practical Justice a verdict in the case of Bry Gilchrist had long since been delivered: guilty. No appeal process. Sentence: whatever was swift, retributive and docket-clearing—mercy a non-starter.

Their eyes met. Hannay's were deeply set and should have been attractive, but they were not. Opaque, she thought, expressing nothing. His smile, however—thin, cold, perceptive—told her he knew what she wanted from him and that he had prepared his defences.

'Mrs Horowitz,' he said suddenly, 'rather to my astonishment, I seem to be experiencing a rush of admiration for you. You are the stuff of team-players. A partisan. A loyalist. I like that, of course. Unfortunately, it is a case of loyalty misplaced.'

'I know you think so,' Helen said.

Reaching for the MacArthur pipe, he tapped it gavel-like on the desk. 'Judge Hannay's Court is now in session.' Jocular, well-disposed. Clearly enjoying himself, he reversed the pipe and aimed it at her. 'The wife of a disenchanted husband is found smothered to death with a pillow. Do *you* need to hear from *me* how often disenchanted husbands and murdered wives make a match? Of course not. At any rate no one's prints on the pillow but his and hers. No alibi that can be corroborated. What *can* be corroborated, however, by four to six unimpeachable witnesses is the bitter spousal quarrel that took place between them earlier in the day.'

'Bitter?'

'You object to bitter? Delete bitter; quarrel will suffice. We are, after all, talking about a man who ran away. And please, no more claptrap about panic. Whatever his faults, Bry Gilchrist has never struck me as a coward.'

'He's not.'

'Well, then?'

'He thought he saw a lynch mob forming. That's why he ran.'

'Guilt is why he ran, dear lady. Or perhaps we are saying the same thing, in effect. He ran because he understood the evidence. Now you will tell me it is circumstantial, intending in that way to debase it, I know. But in my court circumstantial evidence is quite as damning as any other kind.

'I *see* her in the apartment. I see her face contorted with rage. She is furious with him for what she considers betrayal. Deliberately, he absented himself when he knew how essential, how *talismanic* she considered his presence. His fault entirely that she was humiliated. And we *know* she felt that way, don't we?'

Helen kept silent.

He smiled. 'Yes indeed. The twenty of us who were guests at that post-match press conference heard with our own ears, saw with our own eyes. I noted your presence, dear lady. Did you note mine?'

'You were pointed out to me,' Helen said.

'Oh? By whom?'

'By my husband, as a matter of fact.'

'Pointed out. In what terms, I wonder.'

'As not among Bryant Gilchrist's admirers.'

'Though I am, most sincerely, among your husband's. I have followed his cases with a great deal of interest. Most impressive. He has a keen mind and a pragmatic bent. I firmly believe he would approve Judge Hannay's court.'

'You'd be wrong,' Helen said.

At this curtness, annoyance hardened his glance but for only seconds. He really was good at poker-facing when he took the trouble, she thought. The smile restored, the general expression open and benign, he was a portrait of affability—so convincing, she thought, he might even delude himself. She felt a surge of sympathy for the ultra-loyal Mrs Brent and a wave of relief at not being her colleague.

'I stand corrected,' he said. 'Confirmed bachelor though I am, I recognize and bow before the weight of wifely authority. But we do agree about Mrs Gilchrist, do we not? She was . . . what? . . . on fire?'

'She was upset.'

'Upset? She threatened murder, as I recall.'

'She'd just been beaten and was reacting with a temper tantrum. Words. The kind of wild thing people say sometimes.'

'Wild, yes. And when she flew out of the room none of us were in the least doubt as to her destination. Oh, I know, in someone else's court you could object to that as mere surmise. Not here. Here, the so-called rules of evidence do not apply. They are the fogbanks felons and murderers hide in to elude justice. I have no patience with such rules. In my court there are only Hannay rules, only the truth, in other words, which is always perceivable. And once perceived, always triumphant. May I continue?'

'Go ahead.'

'Fury incarnate, she arrives at the apartment, and the earlier quarrel resumes full force. She accuses, he fends her off, their fight grows in intensity.' He paused, squinted slightly, pulled at his chin, and then dropped his remarkable voice to an Iago-like pitch. 'Perhaps at first he meant only to stifle her *volume*.'

He studied her for reaction, and she allowed him a moment of silent applause. Puffed by that and his own performance, he rapped the desk with his pipe again, a little self-lauding tattoo. 'I charge the jury to find the defendant guilty of first degree murder. No other verdict is possible.'

He sat back, arms folded across his chest. The sunlight glinting on the gold of his cuff links was not brighter than his smile.

'Explain the broken window,' she said. 'Why should Bry have to break a window to gain entry to his own apartment? And if he didn't break it, who did?'

'A mysterious intruder,' Hannay said drily. 'Or perhaps someone interested in creating the idea of a mysterious intruder. I'm very much afraid, dear lady, that Bry *did* break his own window. Not to gain entry but to gain a scapegoat.'

'Why is it so hard to believe in a murderer getting in that way?'

The bright smile turned cut-and-thrust. 'Clearly, for some of us, it isn't.'

'Who undressed her?' she asked.

'Oh, please. What difference does it make?'

'Humour me.'

'He undressed her, intending to . . . have his way with her. Or, I suppose it's possible she stripped herself. From all reports that would not have been inconsistent behaviour.'

'*Did* he have his way with her?'

Yawning for effect. 'Probably.'

'No semen,' Helen reminded.

'Ah, the Defence works on its fogbank. My dear lady, I thought I had established my position. In this court there is no such thing as reasonable doubt.'

'Still, it's interesting, don't you think? What's also interesting is the manner in which the police got the report.'

'Conventional behaviour from some public-spirited citizen.'

'Who wouldn't leave a name? And who disguised his or her voice?'

'In what way is that remarkable? He or she didn't want to become more involved than necessary.'

'Or maybe there was an axe to grind.'

'Such as?'

'Framing Bryant. I mean, consider how fast the word came in. Within minutes . . . no more than ten or fifteen after the fact. Sooner, maybe, the medical examiner says. Doesn't that make you wonder a bit?'

Hannay shrugged. 'I like the homely force of, if it looks, walks, and quacks like a duck, that's undoubtedly what it is. Which is to say that if the evidence points overwhelmingly to a man's guilt . . .' He let his voice drift off.

She got to her feet. She walked purposefully towards the door. When she got there, however, she stopped abruptly.

He watched her, warily now.

'The thing is, I've got a problem,' Helen said.

He kept silent.

'Bry said you called him that Friday night and told him Norma Braun left a note addressed to him. I'd like to see it.'

'You can't. No one can.'

'What does that mean?'

'Why, it means there was no such call and no such note. When I confirmed this to your estimable husband he seemed to believe me.'

'Bry's lying?'

'Of course.'

'Most people who know him wouldn't describe him as a liar.'

'Would they have described him as a murderer? No. But we now know he is.'

'You destroyed the note, didn't you?'

'What an absurd concept—the destruction of something that never existed. Still, for the sake of argument, let us say there was such a note. Would it change things materially? How could it? No one saw him at the hospital, no one saw him anywhere.'

'The note would help,' she said.

'In what way?'

'It would give Bry's story ballast. It would add credibility. If they had the note the police might view him differently. And take it from one who's been there—the way the police view you matters.'

'Differently, you say. By that you mean more sympathetically, I suppose.'

'Yes.'

He stroked his perfectly trimmed moustache and smiled his cruelly perceptive smile. 'Mrs Horowitz, no one saw Bryant at the hospital because he was not there to be seen. That is the alpha and the omega of it. Why, then, should I want him viewed more sympathetically?'

She stared at him. 'I think you've done this kind of thing before,' she said.

'What kind of thing would that be?'

'Played God.'

'Ah, I do believe I see what you mean. You mean that if one takes command of events—snatches control from the self-indulgent hands of the crypto-liberal so that the right-thinking are protected, justice served, and chaos averted—that one plays God. Well, I have a less pejorative phrase for it. I call it accepting responsibility. And yes, dear lady, I *have* done it before and stand ready to do it again. There! Another moment of candour for Mrs Brent to swear into oblivion.' He rose and quick-marched to the door, throwing it open. 'And now, good day. Mrs Brent, if this woman ever sets foot in my office again, call the police at once, do you hear?'

'Yes, sir.'

But when he tried to slam the door, she leaned her shoulder against it, forestalling him. He glared up at her, murder in his eyes, and yet he was not sure enough of his capabilities to take a stab at shoving her away. She bowed herself out, shutting the door with infuriating gentleness.

As triumphs went, it was small potatoes, but she revelled in it.

Mrs Brent was making yuk-yuk noises deep in her throat when Helen reached her desk.

'We call him Jengy,' she said. 'For Genghis Khan, you know.'

'Why don't you quit?'

'I have a boy in his sophomore year here. Tuition-free.'

Helen sighed, nodded, and left as Hannay screamed for Mrs Brent's ultra-loyal services.

CHAPTER 2

Seated at his kitchen table, Jacob sipped after-dinner coffee and reread the blistering, entirely irresponsible editorial from that morning's Tri-Towns *Courier*:

THE UN-HUNTING OF BRYANT GILCHRIST

Where *is* Professor Gilchrist? They un-seek him here, they un-seek him there, the Mayor un-seeks him everywhere. Is he in heaven, or is he in hell, the Mayor knows, but he won't tell.

At least that's the sub rosa speculation we hear around Tri-Towns Hall, speculation about a heavy political deal having gone down.

It seems that Gilchrist is connected where it's useful to be connected—that is, to certain international banking fortunes. And that favours have been promised for favours performed.

What kind specifically? Our deep-throaters aren't saying, but did you ever hear of an un-investigation? That's where the police sort of un-hunt for the fugitive involved —un-hunting and un-searching long enough for the public to get preoccupied with all manner of other stuff.

The theory is, you see, that we, the public have short attention spans. And that by the time our minions of the law get around to catching said fugitive—if they ever do —we'll sort of collectively scratch our pointy heads and say: 'That nice man with the amiable smile? Who'd he ever hurt?'

Mayor Knudsen, have you made a deal? Are you in fact un-hunting and un-searching? Say it ain't so.

Prove it ain't so.

Turn loose your Keystone Kops and *find* Bryant Gilchrist. Baby Robin Cantrell was a national treasure. The very least she deserves is justice.

Jacob let the newspaper fall to his lap, experiencing a rare moment of fellow feeling for Sven Knudsen, who earlier in the day had expressed his wholehearted disenchantment with the US Constitution's first amendment.

'And who the fuck says freedom of the press is such a good goddam thing? A bunch of pinko-radical queers, that's fuckin' who.'

Roused by his own rhetoric, the Mayor had prowled the perimeter of Commissioner McCracken's sumptuous office (decorated for him by his profoundly sybaritic second wife), stopping just short of demanding the arrest of Howie Brock, the *Courier's* editor and publisher.

Or probably it just seemed that way. Knudsen, after all, had been Tri-Towns mayor going on sixteen years. You don't hang up that kind of incumbency record, Jacob knew, by ignoring the lesson of John Peter Zenger.

On the other hand, as a conduit for passing pressure along, ranting and raving had always served his honour well. Ranting and raving, and ripping the offending editorial into confetti-like shreds. And rolling the remainder of the newspaper into a club so it could be hammered down on chairs occupied by uncomfortable underlings—namely Police Commissioner McCracken and the homicide squad's Captain Cox. For reasons best known to the Mayor, Jacob's chair went unthreatened.

'Well, I want action, too, by God,' Knudsen had thundered. 'And if I don't get it . . .' Retribution too awful for mere words.

Stocky, florid, with Scandinavian in his colouring and crazed Viking in his eyes, he clomped from the room. Followed hurriedly by the pouter-pigeon form of Liam McCracken in whom sycophantism was not only a matter of practical politics but a calling.

Dennis Cox had then turned his thin, dark face and trapped eyes on Jacob. He looked like a poet whose doomsday vision had suddenly shot into the ascendancy, or like a man in love with the idea of retirement, contemplating twenty-plus years still to go.

'Christ,' he said, 'that's about as berserk as I've ever seen him. I mean, I've seen him when I thought he'd inched over into madness. But never as all-out as this. You, Jacob?'

'No.'

'At the risk of belabouring the obvious, I'd say the case is getting to him.'

'Getting to us all,' Jacob said, who hadn't quite realized until that moment how true it was.

'Yeah,' Cox said. But then he grinned. 'God, I thought it was a woodpecker in here until it came to me it was the Commissioner's knees knocking.' The grin faded. 'Jacob, how can a rank amateur disappear that way? Two weeks now, and it's like Gilchrist fell off the face of the earth. Somebody's got to be hiding him.'

Jacob nodded.

'So who?'

Jacob shut his eyes, as if either a headache or life were causing him pain. When he opened them he said, 'Once, when he was playing in this club tournament and made a dumb move, a game-losing move, Bry Gilchrist got up, took a step backwards, and kicked over a chessboard. I was sitting at the next table. His king landed in my lap.'

'Man has a temper,' Cox said.

'Man has more of a temper than some people are willing to admit,' Jacob said. 'Now, I don't claim that makes him a murderer. I don't say that for a minute. But he's not the junior rabbi some people make him out to be. Facts are facts no matter how much some people don't want to recognize them.'

Cox's silence was thoughtful. After a moment, gaze deliberately averted, he said, 'Helen don't want to recognize them?'

No response.

'Jacob . . . ?'

Breath expelled wearily. 'She got a call from Bry last night.'

Cox nodded.

Jacob looked at him. 'You're not keeling over in a dead faint?'

'If I were a Bryant Gilchrist and was close buddies with a Helen Horowitz that's what I'd have done. He hired her?'

'Yeah.'

'He get himself a lawyer, too?'

'Not yet, I gather.'

'He better. The shit he's in grows deeper by the day.'

Jacob kept silent.

'I don't suppose Gilchrist told Helen where we could locate him?'

'No.'

Cox spent extra seconds inspecting perfectly acceptable fingernails. 'If he'd told her she'd sure as hell pass the information on,' he said.

No response.

'Jacob?'

'You asked and you answered. What do you want from me?' He stood. 'Let's get out of here. God, how I hate a pretty office.'

But Cox pointed at the seat Jacob had just vacated and Jacob, sour-faced, dropped back into it. 'Talk to me,' Cox said.

'Nothing to talk about.'

'You and Helen had words about this case?'

'What kind of words?'

'I'm asking.'

Jacob lifted scuffed black loafers to the highly polished surface of Commissioner McCracken's desk. They then became the only items marring its shiny expanse. 'We didn't exactly have words,' he said. 'We didn't exactly come to an understanding, either.'

'Client goddam privilege,' Cox said, a disdainful snort. 'I knew there'd be trouble about that some day. She's such a hardhead. I should never have let her quit. Your fault, too, Jacob. You encouraged her. She was a great juvenile cop. Letting her go was a screw-up. What are you staring at?'

'You.'

'Well, cut it out. I don't like it. And it doesn't change the truth, which is we *should* have stopped her. And could've, if we'd had an ounce of backbone between us.'

'This is Helen Bly Horowitz you're talking about?'

'She's human, just like anybody else.'

'Only when she wants to be,' Jacob said.

'I'll tell you what, then. What I might do, then, is drag her in here and sweat her a bit. See how she feels about client goddam privilege after a couple or three hours in—'

He broke off, aware of the sudden drop in the room's temperature. There was a coinciding surge of heat to his temples.

'Jesus, listen to me,' he said. 'It's the case, this rotten case. And that ball-busting Knudsen. Jesus, Jacob, I don't believe that came out of me.'

The ice in Jacob's eyes melted slowly, but it melted. When at length the thaw was complete he retrieved a mashed, not unduly clean hat from beneath his chair and placed it over his eyes. Slumping so that in effect he was sitting on his spine, he extended massive legs as far into the room as they would go. Nervously, Cox took a file to his fingernails.

'You won't tell Helen, will you?' he said. 'What I mean is, hell, you know how I feel about her.'

'Secret's safe.'

'Good. Thanks.'

Jacob grinned. 'Because if I told her it wouldn't be me you'd have to worry about, it'd be her. And then it'd take God and two policemen to keep you alive.'

Cox smiled, too, though the effort showed.

They were silent again. Cox put away his nail file and said, 'What did Howie Brock mean about Gilchrist and international banking connections, do you know?'

Jacob nodded. 'Howie and Clara Brock had dinner at our place a month or so ago. Bry was there. He told this nice story about an old uncle he'd gone to visit, an expatriate living in a small town in Italy, near Florence, I think it was. He'd been a fairly big time Boston banker, this uncle, but he got so he hated the business. One day he packed it all in, converted everything he owned to cash and took off, like Gauguin, you know? Only not quite the South Seas. Anyway, living in this little town he found they really needed a bank, the farmers and small business folk. So he opened this one-horse lending institution to make money available at practically no interest. Became a town hero. Howie Brock's got a fertile brain.'

'He's got a brain like a goddam elephant,' Cox said, sighing. 'He just never *is* going to forget who kept him off the ticket and out of the state legislature sixteen years ago. He bashes Knudsen every chance he gets, and guess who's always in the middle—the Keystone Kops, of course. Pricks, the both of them, if you ask me.' He thought about that for an unrewarding moment and then said, 'Put 'em both in a room, 38s drawn, which would you want to see come out?'

While Jacob was pondering, Commissioner McCracken returned. He eased his soft bulk into his cushioned chair. He glanced at the intrusive size eleven and a halfs on his desk, and from those to their owner. When nothing happened as a result, he sent his gaze around the richly appointed office, taking stock as if the contents were at risk and then said, 'Sven's really pissed, boys.'

Cox and Jacob stared at him wordlessly.

Commissioner McCracken—though far from an acute man—knew that his second in command, Cox, and his star investigator, Jacob, were equally convinced of his ineptitude. Nor was the Commissioner disposed to quarrel with this assessment. He merely regarded it as irrelevant.

What signified is that he was where he was because twenty years ago he had tied his fortunes to Sven Knudsen's coat tails, a pivotal decision. Every good thing in his life stemmed from it. Not only his plush office, but his fine suburban house, his two expensive cars, his children's private school education, and his own sartorial splendour.

Indirectly at least, his nubile young wife—to whom he was sexually enslaved—was also a gift from the revered Knudsen. She was drawn to power and thought McCracken had some.

To McCracken, Knudsen was nothing short of godlike. From time to time it penetrated even his under-active sensibilities that Knudsen-worship was not everyone's religion of choice. So be it. He was prepared to tolerate a multiplicity of creeds as long as he was allowed to follow his.

'You have to arrest him, boys. Gilchrist, I mean,' he said. 'The Mayor and the district attorney have conferred, and as of five minutes ago the charge is first degree.'

'One question, sir,' Cox said. 'Do you happen to know where Gilchrist is?'

'Now cut that out. Sven doesn't like that jokey stuff, and you know he doesn't. So no more fooling around.'

Jacob rose and began moving to the door.

'Jacob?' McCracken's tone was full of appeal.

'Jacob doesn't know where to find him, either, ' Cox said, 'but not to worry, he's going to do the next best thing.'

The hope in McCracken's face burned brighter. 'Are you, Jacob? What?'

'He's going to bust up Howie Brock.'

Leaving the *Courier* on the table—folded to Brock's editorial for Helen's perusal—Jacob moved into the living-room. He was beginning to get nervous about her. She was at a dinner-meeting with her office staff and not more than twenty minutes late, but he didn't really like it when she was only five. Which was absurd, since he knew how well she could take care of herself.

He fiddled with the radio a bit, found a Mozart piano concerto, and stretched out on the sofa, kicking off his loafers. After a while Bry Gilchist came into his mind.

Though it still wasn't easy to view Bry as a murderer, it had dropped down a notch from unthinkable. And, in the absence of terrific alternatives, it was getting ever more thinkable, he had to admit. Not that there weren't other *possibilities*; there were, but none that fitted with such custom-made smoothness. For instance:

Ramirez was a rejected lover and Boswell a jealous one, and though neither had a worthwhile alibi (hotel room, early to bed, both, and both unverified) neither could be placed on the spot.

When interviewed by Jacob, young Hattie Lockridge hadn't bothered to hide her dislike of Robin but claimed she'd remained in the field house after the match, practising serves. No corroboration, thus no alibi, but nothing to connect her to the murder scene either.

Sherry Cantrell had gone to the movies. She'd been in one of those moods, she'd said, where she simply hadn't wanted to be with anyone she knew. The movies had seemed to make sense as an answer. Return engagement of *Gone with the Wind*, a film she adored. No ticket stubs, nothing else in the way of verification. On the other hand, no motive that Jacob knew of, though blood relatives were blood relatives and further investigation might turn up something adequate, he acknowledged.

Twenty-five hundred people—including both Horowitzes—had seen Vera Menchicov auction off Baby Robin's Wimbledon racket (championship #4) at almost the exact moment Baby Robin was getting snuffed.

And then of course there was the famous broken window, or the theory that person or persons unknown bore responsibility for Robin's murder, leading directly to the counter-theory that clever Bry had broken the window himself. Leading directly to what Jacob had begun to think of as the Hannay Hypothesis, which he now found himself reviewing.

When Bryant hadn't materialized at her tennis match, Robin, burned up, had gone after him. Arriving at the apartment to find him absent, she had let herself in, deciding in her own inimitable fashion that a Baby in the buff might have certain advantages no matter how the scene played itself out. Mother naked, she had slipped into bed to wait, having first opened and then consumed much of a bottle of scotch to quench her fires and speed the minutes.

Bry, however, had been less pleased to find her there than she'd hoped, buff or not. A quarrel had followed, explosive enough to trigger aberrant behaviour. No relatively harmless open-handed smack this time. Instead, he had, in a moment of escalating and uncontrollable rage, grabbed a pillow and smothered his liquored-up, more or less helpless former mate. After that, horrified and panicked, he had run. Now with bandaids such as his Norma Braun story and his broken window/mysterious stranger(s) story he was desperately trying to patch up his defences.

As hypotheses went, the Hannay was persuasive—simple, uncluttered, workable. No obvious flaws. Nothing that needed wrenching in order to fit the known facts. Against this, Bry's version seemed meagre and ineffectual.

After changing his tyre, Bry said, he had arrived at his apartment to find a naked Baby in his bed. Yes, they had quarrelled but *not* violently. Well, all right, semi-violently; enough so that he had stormed from the apartment, ordering Robin to vacate it by the time he returned. Half an hour, he had given her. Time enough for her to organize (a) a cab, or (b) Boswell, he had said. This was at approximately eleven-thirty. Shortly after midnight he had returned to find her dead.

Of *course* his fingerprints were on the pillow. How could they not be? It *was* his home, after all. Did Bry, then, have an alternative candidate to suggest, Jacob had asked. No, but broken window aside for a moment, Jacob should understand that his and Robin's were not the only keys to the apartment. Who else had them? Bry couldn't say, though it was his conviction that Robin had distributed liberally. And then Bry had hung up, moments before Jacob's tracing effort could become effective.

Persuasive? Hardly. Still . . . a few new facts unearthed, a critical lie or two exposed, an unbreakable alibi suddenly smashed and in the end Bry's version might turn out to be unvarnished truth. Jacob knew it could work that way, but at this point belief in Bry demanded an act of faith. Those came hard to him.

Jacob sighed heavily. What bothered him most about the Hannah Hypothesis—come on, admit it—was Hannay himself. He didn't like the pompous little bastard. Parenthetically, he wondered how Helen's meeting with him had gone, grinning a bit because she suffered twits even less patiently than he did.

But Hannay's charm quotient was hardly the issue here.

Was it? What mattered was that the damn hypothesis seemed to grow more airtight every time you searched it for holes. Having reached this inhospitable way station for the dozenth time that day, Jacob, glum, decided to pour himself some scotch.

He sipped. With the toes of his right foot he located and then manipulated the radio's volume dial to raise Mozart's decibel level. And thought about last night's debate. Restrained and civilized, it had none the less underscored the schism between the Horowitzes. As schisms went, it was modest, sure, but Jacob hated it being there at all. Schisms of any kind had not been common in their eight-year marriage. And this one, he felt intuitively, was a crack reaching for chasm status.

He sat up, placing his glass on the coffee table with more force than he'd intended. Damn, but she could be irritating. How could she not see that 'client privilege' had to have limitations?

He heard her at the door, and a moment later she was on her knees before him, nuzzling his neck. But he held her away so that he could study her. He was pretty sure he'd glimpsed guilt gremlins making themselves scarce in the hollows under her eyes. He waited.

'I can fool almost everyone else,' she said, surrendering.

'Give,' he said.

'I have to drive down to Jekyll Island tomorrow morning. But I'll be home before you know it,' she said, getting it out in a burst.

'Where the hell's Jekyll Island? How long is before I know it? And who's down there that's so important?'

'Not Bry Gilchrist, if that's what you're thinking.'

'No?'

'I swear. And as for the rest of it, Jekyll is one of those coastal islands in the south Atlantic. Off Georgia. Real pretty, I've been given to understand by Marla who used to go there a lot as a child.'

Marla Phipps was Helen's right hand at Bly Investigations, a lively, pretty Vietnam war widow who, like

Helen, was an ex-cop. A compulsive reader, she knew something about an impressive range of subjects. Equally important, from a tactical standpoint, Jacob approved of her. Which meant that on matters sensitive Helen could quote her with impunity.

Jacob's mutter was noncommittal.

Helen peered into his near empty glass. 'Refill?'

'Short.'

She poured for both and seated herself on the sofa next to him, draping his arm around her. 'Some tennis people go there every year around this time to sort of hide out between tournaments.' She hesitated but only briefly. 'Bry told me.'

His mood was not noticeably improved.

'Hide on Jekyll,' she said, poking him.

'Which people?'

'Like Vera Menchicov, for instance. And Tom Boswell, for instance. And like that J. T. Ramirez, maybe.' She swung around to look at him full. 'Jacob dearest, I do have to go.'

He kept silent.

'If the shoe were on the other foot . . . ?'

He took the glass from her and kissed her mouth hard. 'Kill me, the goddam house feels empty already.'

Lifting his hand, she eased it into her blouse. 'Upstairs, my love,' she said, 'is where the killing fields are.'

They'd both been quiet for a while, but he knew from the sound of her breathing that she wasn't quite asleep. He said, 'What time are you leaving?'

Her eyes came open like heavy windows. After a moment she said, 'Early.'

'What's early?'

'I'll set the alarm for four, beat the traffic out of the Tri-Towns. About a ten-, twelve-hour drive thereabouts, Marla says. If I'm tired I'll lay over in North Carolina maybe.'

'You won't be tired. I know you, you'll keep on driving. You drive like a goddam cowboy.'

'Like a goddam Indian. Please.'

'Why don't you take someone from the office with you? Take Marla.'

'She's tailing some deadbeat husband tomorrow.' Her fingers picked a path through the rainforest on his chest. 'Why don't I take you?'

He shook his head. 'Thought about it for a moment, but it'd mean leaving the Captain on his own with Sven Knudsen breathing fire. Can't you just hear Knudsen on desertion and betrayal? Dennis wouldn't be able to cope.'

'Jacob, Jacob, when are you going to listen to your better half?'

'Some day.'

'We could make such beautiful music together. And get rich. I'll put your name up in lights, even put it up there first—Horowitz and Bly, Supersleuths, Inc. No stopping us, my dearest boy. And then we'd never again have to worry about low-lifes like Sven Knudsen. Or fools like Liam McCracken. And we could even find a nice place for useful citizens like Dennis Cox. Say yes, Jacob. It's one, short, terrific word.'

'Some day soon, I promise,' he said, wondering why some day wasn't now and having no real answer to the question which was being raised, he couldn't help noticing, with increasing frequency. She was looking at him oddly, in a way that suggested she might know what he didn't. And that though she didn't much like whatever the answer was, she was prepared to be a good guy and not beat him over the head with her tomahawk, at least not for a moon or so.

Drowsiness routed, she then told him in detail of her meeting with Hannay. 'There *was* a note, Jacob,' she said, finishing. 'You better believe the son of a bitch destroyed it.'

'So what?'

'What do you mean, so what?'

'I don't see it as that important. Note or no note. Bry's hung out there without an alibi.'

She got up on an elbow. 'You've gone a little distance

since last we met, haven't you? Yesterday you were only leaning. Today you'd arrest Bry and throw away the key.'

'I'd have no choice. About arresting, I mean.'

'Oh God, they've gone and issued a warrant?'

He nodded.

She made her Apache spitting noise. 'I hate those no-goods at Tri-Towns Hall. They don't care what they do, or who they do it to. Politics, that's all they care about. Save our sacred skins, ever the name of the game. Guilt? Innocence? Go away, kid, you bother me.'

'You could be wrong, you know.'

'Not about those low-lifes.'

'I mean about Bry. He had motive, opportunity, and he lit out.'

'Because he was scared silly.'

'Damn it, there are things in his story that aren't as locked in as they ought to be.'

'Since when do things have to be that locked in? You're the one who always insists that too smooth smells bad. Like what, for instance?'

He cast about for a point-scoring answer. 'Like why so late with that mysterious intruder theory, for instance. Not a word about it the first time he called. The first time he mentioned mysterious intruder was the second time.'

Aware of the tangle, he started to grin, but she didn't so he left the mess unsorted.

'Jacob, are *you* saying Bry broke the window himself?'

'He could have.'

'Repeat: *Is* that what you're telling me?'

Now he was irritated enough to want to say yes, but he couldn't. The fact was he'd believed Bry's unhesitating impassioned denial when he, Jacob, had bluntly put the question to him. And, sure, he'd been fooled once or twice by unhesitating impassioned denials, but only from John Gielgud-type performers. Bry didn't have that in him. So Jacob kept silent.

'Mule.'

'All right, *maybe* he didn't break the window himself.'

'Thank you for small favours.'

'Person or persons unknown *may* have broken the window.'

'Jacob, if you grant that—'

'*May* have, *may* have. Don't go putting words in my mouth.'

'What happened, of course, is that while Bry was gone, the killer broke in—'

'The killer didn't have a key?'

'The killer might have had a key and lost it. Or not have been carrying it that night. Or, right, might never had had one. At any rate, the killer breaks in, does Robin, takes off. Bry comes home, finds her, and when he realizes she's dead he—'

'Panics. I know. As a result of which he can't think straight, talk straight, or do anything else that might have kept him out of deep shit.'

'God, you sound like Hannay the Hangman.'

'And you, if you don't mind my saying so, sound less like a cop than you ought to. Evidence, shmevidence. Intuition, that's what matters. What you sound like, Mrs Horowitz, is an Apache whatchamacallit stirring eye of newt in a cauldron.'

'Eye of what?'

'Or whatever else you use for double, double, toil and trouble. The thing is, I'm not happy either when it adds up to Bry Gilchrist. He'd have been charged a week ago if it weren't for me. Hell, I like Bry.' The ensuing pause was almost infinitesimal, but, to a pair as attuned to each other as they were, not to be missed. 'Almost as much as you do.'

Her silence after that was prolonged. Jacob didn't much care for the way she was being silent. It made him seriously uncomfortable.

Suddenly there was space between them. No more fingers doing their walking through Horowitzian forests.

'Almost as much as I do? What does that mean?' she asked.

'Nothing.'

'Nothing?'

Such a simple thing to do—say the word again and mean it. Add an endearment for emphasis. Haul her back and squeeze her in friendship or whatever. And in fact nothing *would* be nothing. Most of him wanted it that way, but part of him didn't. And while the inner debate raged she got out of bed. When next he saw her she wore her heavy white bathrobe and was looking remote. The chair she sat in was on the other side of the room and the other side of the world.

'Spit it out, Jacob,' she said. What she didn't say, but what hung in the air like a challenge from some guy who thought you were afraid of him—or so Jacob construed it—was: if you dare.

So Jacob dared. 'Maybe you like him too much,' he said.

'Like him too much. As in maybe I want him in my bed?'

'Do you?'

It seemed to him that her eyes had darkened to blackboard opacity. The room felt thick with the kind of tension you could reach out and break pieces from. He wished he were in Alaska, or anywhere but here. He wished he were back in the land of five minutes ago. And yet nothing could shut his damnfool mouth.

'Do you?' he repeated.

'I wouldn't mind,' she said.

But as she spoke her expression changed. Just for a moment she looked frightened and young and heartbreakingly vulnerable. He was out of bed and hugging her.

'I'm a jackass.'

But the moment had gone and forgiveness with it. Her body remained stiff, resistant. She got free of him. 'Jacob, do me a favour, please.'

He waited, certain of one thing—how much he was going to hate this favour.

'I don't want to be disturbing you at four in the morning, so—'

'You won't disturb me.'

'So please sleep in the den tonight.'

'Helen—'

'Just for tonight, please.'

Circumstances had placed miles between them from time to time, but never while under the same roof had they slept apart. Jacob's stomach had knots in it.

'Maybe you're making too big a thing of this,' he said.

She kept silent.

'I mean, maybe you're angrier than you should be.'

'How angry should I be?'

'I said I was a jackass. That's an apology.'

'Yes.'

'You want more? You want me to beg?'

'No.'

'Then maybe you could try and be a little less angry.'

'I am trying. I'm trying like hell. And it's not doing much good right now. And so I'd like you to please sleep in the den tonight.'

'I see.'

She drew the lapels of her robe up around her neck. She looked cold. A different kind of cold was in her face. Or maybe the same kind, he thought.

'And tomorrow night you won't be here,' he said.

'No.'

'And that's OK with you?'

'Yes.'

He found blanket, sheets and pillows and carried them downstairs. She watched him, making no move to help. When he awoke in the morning she was gone. No note.

CHAPTER 3

Jacob turned the key in the lock, opened the door to Bryant Gilchrist's apartment and heard music coming from the bedroom, a Beethoven symphony, the seventh, he thought. Also wafting towards him was the distinctive smell of woodsmoke.

He shut the door, and, having tracked sound and scent to their sources, was at least mildly surprised to come upon Vera Menchicov in a chair by the fireplace.

She didn't glance up at his entrance. Her face had that raptness people get when the fire gods have hypnotized them. The blaze crackled; she studied it; he studied her.

In a form-hugging navy blue jersey dress she looked more like something out of *Vogue* than *Sports Illustrated*. A white cloth coat with scallops of navy fur trimming the neck, cuffs, and hem was slung across the bed. Her long, stockinged (maybe panty-hosed, navy at any rate) legs were crossed. In tennis dress they had never seemed so riveting.

Still without glancing up, she said, 'I thought it might be you, Lieutenant. The Barkers told me you'd been hanging round the scene of the crime.'

The Barkers were the elderly, gossipy live-in couple who looked after the building. 'They gave you a key?' he asked.

'They didn't have to.'

'No?'

Now she glanced up and smiled. 'But that's not really news to you, is it? Have you so soon forgotten my command performance at your snug little office? Surely not. It was only last week. Don't you remember, you took a rubber hose to me, and I told you Baby bestowed keys on her best buddies, which means half the tennis tour.'

'The final count seems to be four.'

'Four? I don't believe it. You checked *everybody* out?'

'Everybody we could think of.'

'Ah, but somebody may have lied to you.'

'Somebody always does.'

She made a *moue* of false sympathy and jeering amusement.

He said nothing, watching her, thinking that the word she had used just now—performance—was basic to the way she lived and breathed. She was all theatricality, he thought, bravura gestures, hokey poses, but always in-your-face, as if it didn't matter in the least whether the bag of tricks stayed hidden or not. The fun was in the doing of it, *her* fun, and let the beholder beware. She caught him studying, and stuck her tongue out.

'What happened to the Russki accent?' he asked.

'That old thing? Comes and goes, depending on mood or need. Bet you didn't know Baby could do accents, too. You should have heard *her* Russian princess. About ten times broader and funnier than mine. Baby could do anything once she decided she wanted to.' She paused and then added something under her breath that Jacob barely caught. 'Except stay alive, the bitch.'

The flames had snared her again, and she watched entranced. Patiently, Jacob set himself to outwait the spell.

At length she looked up, her smile self-mocking. 'If you want to know the truth I thought *I* had the only duplicate key. The more fool me, right?'

'You sound . . . resentful.'

'And you sound like a cop with a bug up his asski.'

Her glance, swinging towards him had changed sharply in quality. She studied him this way and that for a while but then relaxed—sighed and shrugged.

'Baby was so damned indiscriminate. She—' She broke off, shook her head and then said, 'Even dead she has a knack for—' Again she broke off. She smacked her cheek, a smart little wallop, and stood up, striding to the bed for her coat. 'God, listen to me,' she said. 'I'm beginning to spook myself. I've been sitting here for three hours, worshipping at the shrine. That's long enough, wouldn't you say?' She didn't wait for him to answer. Instead, she cupped a hand around her mouth and shouted, 'Bye-bye, Baby, wherever you are. Consider yourself exorcised.' Like a seal coming out of water, she shook herself hard. After a moment she turned back to Jacob. 'You think I'm nuts? Maybe I am. Still, I feel like I just got something out of my system. So long, comrade.'

Without seeming to hurry he got to the door before she did. She was impressed. 'How did you do that?'

'Do what?'

'Move that hulk of a body of yours so fast? How'd you like a mixed doubles partner name of Menchicov?'

'Aren't you supposed to be on Jekyll Island?' he asked.

'You're keeping tabs? Not that I'd mind, you understand —big, strong studski like you. The thing is, I was under the impression you already had your murderer. Didn't I read this morning about a hue and cry?'

'You think that's a mistake?'

She poked a long but delicately made finger at her pleasantly rounded chest. '*Moi?* I'm a tennis player, dearie. What do I know about crime and punishment? Can I go now?'

'Where to?'

'Again I ask—official or un? The thing is, I'm getting the feeling it might be the former. What's going on here, Lieutenant? Is there, or is there not a warrant out for Bry Gilchrist's arrest?'

'There is.'

'So you're just curious, is that it?'

'It might be.'

'Then fuck off.' She slapped his hand away from the door knob and pulled the door open. He made no attempt to detain her, but halfway through she stopped anyway. 'Sorry about that. Believe it or not, I hate being rude.' She smiled. 'Especially to cops. Where to, you asked? To Jekyll, where else? A day or so late but better late than never, I always say. To Jekyll, where, surrounded by peace, quiet, and the solacing of good friends I will recover my equanimity.'

'Good friends?'

'You would like me to enumerate? Well, then: Ramirez, Boswell, and Sherry Cantrell.' She drew an airy circle which included herself. 'The four musketeers.' A thought seemed to strike. 'The four key-holders, am I right?'

'Yes.'

'Can you make something of that, Lieutenant?'

He kept his expression noncommittal.

'You're not sure, but you might be willing to try?'

'What will you be doing on Jekyll?' he asked.

'I told you, we'll horse around, play a bit of hit and giggle, eat, sleep, be blithe spirits. It's a ritual, something Baby started five, six years ago for a select group of her fellow gypsies. A long Friday to Monday weekend, for which she'd pick up the tab. How else shall I put it? A time-warp kind of a thing, just as if there were no such animal as the Grand Slam Monster straddling our lives. Know what I mean? Of course you don't. Anyway, she'd set it up somewhat before the Australian Open, sending out printed invitations to half a dozen of us, sometimes a few more: your presence is required on Jekyll for Fuck-Off Time. And that's what would happen. All good fellows together.' She looked at him, her expression suddenly complicated. 'Generally.'

He did what was expected of him and said, 'But sometimes not?'

She glanced down. When he could see her face again it was wonderfully pious. Her eyes seemed much larger, even bluer, he thought—impressed at such virtuosity—and utterly guileless. He thought it was the way they'd appear to an opponent who was about to guess wrong as to which section of the court required coverage.

'There was the time Jatie took a swing at someone, missed, hit the wall, and broke his left wrist. He is a southpaw, you know. He lost four months of the tour that year.'

'Who did he swing at?'

She nipped at her lip, rubbed a knuckle.

'Boswell?' he asked.

'No,' she said and spun away from him to resume her interrupted exit. 'Actually, it was Baby.'

He caught her hand and gently drew her back. 'Why did you tell me that?'

'Why?' Once more she zapped him with lethal blues. 'Because it's the truth, of course.'

He reached over and with his thumb slowly lowered her lids—first one, then the other—holstering weapons. She grinned at him.

'I do like a big-shouldered man,' she said.

He said nothing.

'You're still holding my hand,' she said.

He released it.

'Where were we? Ah yes, seekers after truth. Honestly, do you really believe Bry was the only one Baby ever worked over?'

'If I did up until about two minutes ago, I guess I don't any more.'

'Now, now, let's be careful here, Jacob. All right if I call you Jacob? I meant poor old Jatie only as a case in point. There are others as interesting.'

'Your young friend Hattie Lockridge, for instance?'

She raised an eyebrow.

'I got that wrong? Young Hattie's not your friend?'

'I think you know that, Jacob.'

'Tell me again about the dirty trick you and Robin once played on her.'

She smiled. 'Think back now, Jacob. We're in your little snuggery with the colourful posters on the wall, with the handcuffs dangling from the chair arms. There's your rack and other medieval instruments of torture. There's your blood-and-tearstained desk, and on a corner of it, a photo of that remarkable-looking woman, your wife. And, yes, we hear you querying as to alleged dirty tricks, but do we hear me answering?'

'You couldn't recall, is what you said.'

'Correct.'

'But that pre-dated your conversion.'

'I'm at a loss, Jacob. What conversion is that?'

'To the Judaeo-Christian ethic, truth-speaking in particular.'

She looked at him speculatively. 'You know, I truly believe I could fall in love with a smart-ass like you. Oh well, *l'affaire* Lockridge is certainly no secret. Did you ask around?'

'Yes.'

'And?'

'It's no secret.'

'Ah, but you think it might be different coming from the source? Or maybe you *hope* it'll be different, so you can make me squirm.'

'That wouldn't be easy.'

She contorted her features in a salacious leer. 'You'd be surprised,' she said.

Folding his arms across his chest, Jacob waited.

'Hattie Lockridge hates her mother, did you know that?'

'I'd heard.'

'Actually everybody hates Simone, the bullying bitch. Simone Legreeski, I call her. Last year Hattie kicked her out; that is, wouldn't let her travel with us any more. That took guts. Short on brains, Hattie is, but never on guts. The whole tour celebrated.'

She paused and made a business out of trying to stoke the fire. He took the poker from her. The fire blazed up vigorously, but when he turned towards her again she wasn't even looking at it, and though she gave him her wiseguy smile, it was off a degree, he thought.

'Anyway there was this one dumb day I convinced her that Robin was her real mother, that Jatie was her father, and that Simone had done a scam to steal her from them.'

'Convinced her,' Jacob said after a moment.

Vera nodded.

'I wonder how a body'd go about doing that.'

'It was easy. And I knew it would be. Hattie detests Simone—almost as much as she adored Baby, worshipped her. Tongue-tied and clumsy. Blushes, cow-eyes, and all the rest. The kid was a sitting duck.'

'Terrific stunt,' Jacob said expressionlessly.

'And there you were thinking I was all angel.' She shook her head and sighed. 'I was pissed at the time, of course. Baby, too. She'd been drinking with me to commiserate. Hattie had just whipped me in the first round of the French Open. A fifteen-year-old! *Moi!* I'd never lost in the first round of anything before. You have no idea how dangerous I am when I'm feeling low.

'Anyway it only lasted a day or so, the whole thing. Then I confessed. God, she was sore. Even sorer at Baby than at me, for some reason. And all Baby did was back me up for about fifteen minutes. All right, all right, don't bother to explain. I *know* why she was sorer at Baby. But Baby's dead now, and Hattie still wants my guts for breakfast. She goes around stalking me in that smouldering, sullen way of hers. You'd think a person might forgive and forget after a while. Do some magic with that fire, please. Damn, but it's cold in here.'

He threw a log on. It caught, and she held her hands towards the renewed blaze.

'So Hattie flipped out, you're saying. And sore as a boil, she sent those so-called anonymous notes to Robin.'

'Hattie told you about the notes?'

'I asked, so she told me.'

'How did you know to ask? Wait. You found them in Robin's purse. Of course you did. A rat's nest, that purse. She never threw anything away.' She studied him. 'You thought what we did at first, I'll bet.'

'Which is?'

'That Bry sent them.'

'You don't think so now?'

'No way. Once you get past the May 10th thing that becomes absurd. May 10th? The day Bry turned up where he wasn't supposed to? *Remember May 10th*, one of those notes said, so naturally Bry came to mind. But he really doesn't fit any other way, does he? Not his style at all.' She smiled. 'No literary curlicues. And then Robin had a brainstorm. It suddenly struck her there was something else significant about May 10th.'

It had struck Jacob, too. 'Mother's Day,' he said.

'And things being as they were, that meant Hattie to us.'

'Did you accuse her?'

'Not me, but Robin did. That is, she went to her. Not to accuse, really, but . . . you know . . . to talk about it, sort of. Hattie didn't deny it for a minute. Started screaming about how that was only the beginning of what she intended to do to get back at us lying bitches.'

'When was this?'

'About an hour before the big match that Friday. Hey,

you think it threw the brat off her game? Love and love, as I recall.'

They stared into the fire for a while.

'Jacob . . .'

'What?'

'As you've certainly gathered, I'm not a very serious person. Still . . .' She stopped long enough so that he thought she was going to leave it there, but she didn't. 'What this has been is me trying to tell you I really do want that killer caught.'

'Who you don't think is Bry.'

'No.'

'But who you do think might have been Hattie?'

'Maybe, maybe not. It just seems to me she has more murder in her than Bry does—young as she is. But what the hell, Sherlock dear, why don't you ask her yourself?'

'I have.'

'Well, if you've picked up an insight or two here today, and you want to do it again you can pretty easily. She's in New York, you know. There's a Virginia Slims at the Garden that I skipped out of. Go on up to her and smack her in the teeth with it. "Hattie, baby, do you have murder in your heart?"'

He looked at her.

'I know what you're wondering,' she said. 'You're wondering if there's murder in *my* heart.'

'Why should I be wondering along those lines?'

'Why shouldn't you be?'

'Aren't you the lady with the ironclad alibi?'

She was silent a moment. 'You're not going to find this easy to believe, but damn if I didn't forget about that. But *you* won't, will you?'

'No.'

'And if you suspect there's the tiniest flaw in my precious alibi, you'll make my life miserable until you find it.'

'Nothing personal.'

'I almost feel sorry for me,' she said.

She smiled, but he didn't.

'And *now*,' she said, 'you're wondering about my warning.'

'What warning?'

'When I'm low, I'm dangerous.' Stepping into him before he could stop her, arms about his neck, breasts and thighs pressing hard.

He freed himself.

'Naughty, naughty,' she said, waggling a finger at him, underscoring a shared awareness that he hadn't broken the kiss quite as quickly as he might have. And then she was gone.

Jacob returned to the bedroom, taking the chair Vera had vacated and slipping into her fire-staring mode. Which was she—clever or honest? He thought about it for a while and concluded that the longer you knew her the more conclusions you would be likely to pile up. She didn't really help you much. Seemingly, she *dared* you to distrust her. Or was that some kind of convoluted, high-risk game the Vera Menchicovs of this world obsessively played? I'll *appear* untrustworthy, trusting to you, Sherlock Horowitz, to find me trustworthy, appearances be damned, whereas the truth is I'm as shifty as a Borgia. Ugh.

Was that alibi ironclad? Could it be there was some obvious hole in it, some emperor's-new-clothes aspect that the deep-buried child in Horowitz would spot at once if he could find a way to spring him.

An incipient throb developed over his left temple. He recalled what his grandfather had been fond of saying when human enigma made *him* brain-weary. If an ache, give it a break. Jacob decided that was wisdom, and for the time being shoved Vera and her shockingly soft mouth back into his subconscious with all the rest that was unresolved.

Bry. The room was the essence of him: his books, his pictures, his old-fashioned roll-top mahogany desk, his hand-carved, Staunton-mould chess set. If Jacob were to throw open that closet he would find Bry's ageing but still excellent tweed sports jackets, his flannel slacks, his motley collection of British brogans, his beat-up running shoes.

Because Bry came to life in this room, Jacob had found it easier to focus here. Focus on what? On *the* question, folks —the central, existential one: could Bryant Gilchrist be a murderer? He concentrated on that now, on his not notably savage friend who had sat opposite him during the course of so many chess games. He conjured him up: gentle eyes and sensitive mouth; soft-spoken, understated style, flashes of self-deprecating wit. *And flashes of temper!*

OK, OK. That having been noted, the man was not, damn it, typecast for the rôle.

The flames danced. Jacob's mind leaped and twirled with similar gracelessness. He got the wayward thing under discipline, though the throbbing was for real now, and forced it to its work.

The result was predictable. Dredged up for him were cases in which previously well-behaved citizens suddenly snapped— such as the selfless husband who, after a decade of caring for an invalid wife, had calmly sent her hurtling down the stairs in her wheelchair; the twelve-year-old girl whose vengeance on her mother (a suburban Messalina) took the form of a dozen mortal wounds (sewing scissors), commemorating her birthdays.

Inevitably, then, he was confronted with the formulation he'd been trying to evade. Like so: based on instinct, on experience, on every shred of demographic data generated by the FBI's ever-active computers, Jacob joylessly acknowledged that given the right pressures, the right set of circumstances, anyone can kill.

Aloud, as if to Helen, he announced: 'I don't say absolutely that he did. I only say he could have.' Adding, with something of a snarl, 'That is, I would if I were speaking to you, which I'm not.'

Both youngsters were hard-hitters and enthusiastic grunters, but they didn't have much else in common, Jacob thought: a fire hydrant versus a flagpole. Hattie Lockridge was eight inches shorter than her opponent and outweighed her by 30 pounds. But the most notable difference between the two was about to be demonstrated.

Serving 6-5 for the first set, Hattie walloped one cross-court and came in behind it. Her opponent did well to get her racket in place and actually returned with surprising firmness. Hattie, however, was positioned perfectly for the killing volley. That is, she would have been had the ball not hit the net cord, geysering up and over her poised racket. Blessing her luck and counting the point, her opponent relaxed.

Unlike Hattie who wheeled, took off for the baseline, and arrived not merely in time for the return but for a brutal smash off the high bounce—down the line and miles away from the stunned flagpole: game and set to Miss Lockridge, the small crowd was informed, though it was already reacting at a decibel level that belied its modest size.

Jacob whistled softly.

'Yeah, she's remarkable, isn't she?'

The man who slid into the seat next to him was tall, fortyish, and darkly handsome with an easy way of moving that made observers think of cowboys and wide-open spaces, which amused Jacob since Matty was as city bred as Jacob himself: Matty Mathews, twice US Open champion and Jacob's old friend.[1]

'You can't teach that kind of thing,' Matty said. 'It comes with the fertilized egg. How are you, Jacob?'

Jacob told him, received Matty's updates and managed to keep his expression non-revealing during the up-dates on respective wives.

Among the information bits Matty passed on was the fact that he was this tournament's director. 'Not what you'd call a blockbuster,' he added ruefully, his glance counting a house that could easily hold 15,000 and was accommodating perhaps half. 'Though we might have done a little better if Vera Menchicov hadn't got sick.'

'Sick?' Jacob said, startled.

Matty looked at him for a moment. 'I'm guessing you've

[1] See *Sudden Death*, Jacob Horowitz's first case.

seen her within the past twenty-four hours and that she looked the picture of health. Well, the disease is called The Continental Grippe. It can strike without notice anywhere in the country, afflicting those players who feel like skipping out on a bothersome tournament.'

'I see.'

Matty shrugged. 'On the other hand, the truth is that the guts go out of the game between the US and Australian Opens and there's not much you can do about it but be philosophical. So, Jacob, what the hell are *you* doing here?'

He didn't answer right away. He watched as Hattie, with a second set break point now, suddenly jumped into the alley, daring the flagpole to try for a winner down the middle. She did and double-faulted.

'Pretty savvy stuff,' he said. 'What I am doing here is business, I hope.'

'Baby Robin business?'

'From your mouth to God's ear. Tell me something. Is she a dope?' Indicating Hattie.

Matty reflected. 'Not as smart as you, Jacob, but then with Einstein gone nobody is. No, I'd never say she was a dope. She's a kid with average smarts and a greedy mom who pulled her out of school much too young because she saw the buck in it. So Hattie barely knows who George Washington is and forget asking her to find France on a map of Europe. Still, what she intuits about people will sometimes surprise you.'

'Yeah?'

'Savvy is a word you just used, Jacob.'

'Savvy don't fit with believing that malarkey about Robin being her mother.'

'Oh, that. Hell, Jacob, everybody knows that answer.'

'So include me in.'

Matty smiled. 'She believed what she wanted to, of course.

The woman who answered Jacob's knock could have stepped out of Vera Menchicov's word-portrait of her. She was large and garishly made up. She wore purple sweats with the name Lockridge stencilled across a bulging bosom. Her nose and chin bulged, too, and there was something ungainly about the way she moved, as if the walk, as a method of locomotion, could still surprise her with its complexities. Her eyes, however, seemed to belong in a different person. Her eyes were clever.

'I don't know what you all are pestering us for,' she said, unsheathing her Texas twang. It was sharp and strident, and Jacob knew she enjoyed its abrasiveness. 'We done bared our souls to you over and over. Maybe I should call the police.'

'I am the police,' Jacob reminded mildly as he sidled past her.

'Not here you ain't. Like I said to you over the phone, I got advice. My advice says you're out of your jurisdiction here, sweet thaing.'

'Mama, shut up. Who asked you to butt your two cents in?'

A younger, less strident twang. Hattie Lockridge lay stretched out on a sofa watching television, a soap opera. She, too, wore purple sweats. Her face, however, was devoid of make-up, and there was no fat on her anywhere—just solid, impressive muscle. Still, the family resemblance was not to be missed.

Safely inside now, Jacob glanced about him. The Lockridge suite was spacious and impeccably appointed, almost elegant. Odd that Mrs Lockridge seemed somehow more at home in it than her daughter.

'Thanks for seeing me,' Jacob said. 'I'll try not to take too long.'

Hattie nodded but kept her gaze fixed on the screen, which was now filled by two large heads whose owners were poised to fasten hungry mouths on each other.

'Do you mind if I lower the volume?' Jacob asked.

'Hell, yes, we mind,' Mrs Lockridge said. 'We're watching something. Who the hell are you to come traipsing in here taking over the place? And you ain't even got the jurisdiction.'

Hattie swung her feet off the sofa and zipped across the room to the bedroom door. She opened it. 'Nap time, Mama,' she said.

The older woman became a battlefield. It was easy for Jacob to gauge the progress of the war being fought and know just when rebellion was routed. The brightness of combat dimmed in 'Mama's' eyes and a puff of escaping breath made a noise like a bubble bursting. She left as ordered.

Recalling the status quo Vera had described to him, Jacob wondered if this new one constituted the sole basis on which Mrs Lockridge had been allowed to rejoin her daughter, and thought that more than probable.

Like an animal handler caging one of her charges for the night, Hattie shut the door firmly. She then returned to the sofa, though not before lowering the volume as requested. She sat uncomfortably straight, it seemed to him, watching the TV exercise in mutual engorgement.

'What is it, please?' she asked. 'My mama's right. I did tell you everything I could about . . . you know. And I have practice very soon.'

He took the easy chair opposite her. 'Those notes,' he said.

Her glance remained on the lovers. 'What about them? I sent them because I was mad, and I wanted to get something back for what was done to me. I told you that.'

'But you waited a while, didn't you?'

'Because I couldn't think of anything smart to do. Then I saw this TV movie. It was about these kidnappers? They cut this ransom message out of newspapers? Well, that gave me the idea about the notes, so I sent them.'

'By then almost four months had gone by, isn't that right?'

'I guess.'

'And you hadn't cooled down?'

The longest kiss on record hadn't cooled down either,

and she followed its progress intently while toying with a heavy gold charm bracelet. This featured a cunningly fashioned intermingling of miniature tennis balls and rackets. With her arm as fulcrum, she kept the bracelet careening in a perpetual rollercoaster ride.

'Cooled down? No. And I ain't yet. And I don't plan to ever. What they did to me was rotten.'

The bedroom door was thrown open, and Mrs Lockridge was once more among them. 'Vamoose!' she screamed, indicating the direction with outflung arm. 'Now! I called my advice, and he's on his way over here. And he ain't no small-time piddling pig-shit advice, either. He's connected. And I mean connected every goddam which-away you can think of, so if you ain't out of here in the next minute and a half, sweet thaing . . .'

Hattie rose, crossed the room—this time with ostentatious weariness—corralled her, and herded her back whence she had escaped.

'He's trying to trick you, Hattie baby. He wants you to say something bad so he can . . . Please, honey, let your mama stay so she can . . . *Don't* shut me—'

The door closed behind her.

'She won't come out again,' Hattie said in that quiet, uninflected tone that sounded so completely authoritative. Jacob felt chilled by it. She was too young for it. It was as if a cabal of exploiters had snatched her childhood, depriving her of it so effectively that by now she no longer knew what she missed. Jacob felt sorry for her but understood that was mere sentimentality. She had no use for his sympathy and would not have thanked him for it.

The kissers had disengaged at last, left exhausted and shrunken by the experience. Maybe, as with bees after stinging, osculation would end their lives. Hattie turned the TV set off, returned to her seat and glanced at her watch.

'Ten minutes, and then you have to go,' she said politely.

Having decided to take at least double that for the sake of principle, Jacob was hard put to find uses for even half.

The problem was he couldn't persuade himself there had been good reason to come. Fitfulness had pushed him, an anxiety about unturned stones that was part of his nature, the kind of thing that on the one hand made him good at his job and on the other diminished the pleasure he could take in it.

Attention to detail, Helen termed it when she was pleased with him. Nit-picking, when she was not.

Damn! Just like that she had eluded the sentries guarding his perimeter and was now posted advantageously behind his lines. He had thought her banished for a while. He had worked hard at banishing her. He wondered if her Trip to Bountiful, or Jekyll, or wherever, had been without incident. He wondered if her plans included returning home at some point.

'Sleep-creepin',' Hattie said.

'What?'

'It's me, Hattie Lockridge, who you dropped by to see, only now you're sleep-creepin' around like there's no way you remember. I used to do that some. And then Mama'd crack me, and I sure enough stopped. Mama could crack.'

'She looks like she still can.'

'Does she?' Something happened in Hattie's face that was easier to describe than interpret. Words like powerful and/or implacable came to Jacob's mind. 'Well, that don't matter much now,' Hattie said. 'Nothing about Mama does.'

Suddenly he felt an unexpected weight. Glancing down, he identified the previously flying object as Hattie's charm bracelet, which had swung free and landed on the toe of his shoe. It glittered there for a moment.

'Sorry,' she said.

Carefully, he raised his foot, retrieved the bracelet and gave it to her. 'Do you think Bry Gilchrist murdered Robin?' he asked.

'Why would you ask me? I only met him once or twice.'

'Did you like him?'

She shrugged. 'Too itty-bitty. But I guess for murderin''

that don't really signify, does it? I mean, I guess he could've if he'd wanted to.'

'But he's not your best bet?'

She smiled.

'Why is that funny?'

'This is just like TV. Like *Knot's Landing*, maybe, and you're questioning me, and maybe the audience don't know if I'm telling the truth or not. Well, all right, the truth is Vera's my best bet.'

'Why?'

'Because I hate her.'

'No other reason?'

'And because—' But she broke off. It was her mama's chin that jutted out at him, and he knew he was not going to be able to get her to reveal what she had censored.

But he tried. 'Withholding information from the police is a serious crime, you know. It could land you in plenty of trouble.'

'Could it?'

'It sure could.'

Her smile broadened into a grin. 'But you ain't got the jurisdiction, sweet thaing.'

He grinned, too, though he did his best not to. And his grin made her giggle. For a moment he had the sense of a giddy sixteen-year-old peeping out at him turtle-like. But then she was deep in her shell again. 'I meant that before,' she said. 'I ain't ever going to forgive them.'

'Robin's dead,' he pointed out.

'But Vera ain't.'

They held each other's glances. In his time Jacob had encountered children capable of all the demonism their elders were, every wickedness, transgression, and depravity. If this were such a one, she was a monster camouflaged by fresh skin, clear eyes, and freckles. He saw her shaking her head and knew she had read his thoughts.

'Mister, the only place I kill is on the tennis court,' she said.

*

When the elevator arrived Jatie Ramirez was in it. Jacob stepped back.

Jatie scowled. 'What are you doing here?'

'Making a friendly visit.'

'To whom?'

Though the tone was pugnacious enough, Jacob detected an underlying anxiety. It interested him. He wondered what might be causing it. A moment later, he decided he knew, wondering then if pushing might do some good. Tactics aside, there was something about Jatie that made Jacob naturally think in those terms. He had noticed that during his first interviews with him—a sort of anti-chemistry—and felt it no less palpably now. And felt also, as he had before, that it was certainly mutual.

'Better hurry, or you'll miss her,' he said. 'She's just about ready to leave for practice.'

'Who?'

Jacob smiled as infuriatingly as he could.

Jatie's fists hovered at his sides as if over pistols.

Jacob pressed for the elevator again. 'See you around,' he said. 'I'll tell Vera I ran into you.' Amending that to: 'Where I ran into you.'

The elevator reappeared and Jacob moved towards it. Jatie reached out to stop him. Jacob peered at the offending arm and after a moment Jatie withdrew it.

'I am not a man to mock,' he said.

'The world and his brother know that.'

'People who mock me, who underestimate me, sometimes end by regretting it.'

'As they should.'

Jatie stared at Jacob, but Jacob, bemused by an incipient hangnail on his left pinky, fixed his attention there lest it burst into bloom unwitnessed. Besides, he had little idea as to what might constitute the tactical next step.

'Hattie?' Jatie asked suddenly.

'Was I visiting Hattie? Yes, I was. Which is where you're heading, right?'

'You find that objectionable?'

'Not me.'

Jatie studied him for a moment, then as if satisfied that he had brought about an acceptable degree of behaviour modification, moved off down the hall.

Jacob let him go ten feet or so. 'Hell,' he said, 'maybe it isn't the old double-cross. That's up to Vera to decide, I guess.'

Jatie returned. His eyes glittered like tiny black light bulbs. Confronting each other the two men were almost of a size—Jacob broader, Jatie younger.

'Double-cross?' Jatie's upper lip seemed not to move.

'Maybe, maybe not. What do I know?'

'If I hit you, you will arrest me,' Jatie said.

'If you hit me, I'll kick your teeth in,' Jacob said, 'but I won't arrest you. I don't have the jurisdiction.'

They stared some more. Then Jatie said, 'She is getting ready to betray *me*. I know she is. I am sick and tired of being betrayed.'

'Vera?'

'All of them. Yes, Vera.'

'I'll tell her you said so.'

'Tell her what you like,' Jatie said and turned away.

As Jacob watched his heavy-footed progress—a man who had let pleasure curdle and joy sour—he wondered when it was exactly that Jatie had grown sick and tired of being betrayed.

The following morning, as he crossed from Blaine to Montgomery (smack in the middle of which was the complex of no-nonsense brick buildings that housed Central Police Headquarters, the town council hall, as well as the mayor's office) Jacob heard himself honked at: Howie Beck in his majestic black Lincoln. Beck eased over to the kerb and jabbed something that caused the window closest to Jacob to react electronically.

'Buy you lunch?' he asked.

'No.'

Beck smiled. 'Knudsen's in Chicago on some kind of

mayors' freebie. Won't be back in the Tri-Towns until the weekend.'

In his mid-forties, he was youthfully trim with a shock of white hair that made a spectacular contrast against his suntan, which was perpetual. His clothes, stopping just short of natty, were lovingly tailored. His clothes, his car, everything about him made a statement. In giving me wealth and power, they said, the master planner has ordered things responsibly.

'Come on, come on, Jacob. We'll do it in the Union League. No one there would be caught dead talking to Sven Knudsen, much less informing to him. Hop in.'

'I'll see you there at one,' Jacob said and resumed his march.

At his office he found three messages: one from Chief McCracken, one from Captain Cox, and one, long-distance, from a woman who hadn't left her name but said she'd call back. Certain this meant a contrite Helen, Jacob's spirits soared and remained aloft until young Mary Peroni, the officer Cox had recently detailed to him as adjutant, poked her head in and clipped his wings.

'Fiftyish, deep husky voice. She wouldn't talk to anyone else.'

Jacob made one last scenario-saving attempt. 'She didn't sound like anyone you know?'

Mary looked blank.

'I mean, like anyone from around here?'

'It was a long-distance call. Didn't I say?'

'I mean, like Helen maybe, with a cold or an allergy?'

'Helen? No, sir. Not the least little bit,' she said and left after noting his appointment with Beck on the calendar she kept for him.

Jacob tried to recall a pertinent Apache swear word or two. He couldn't. Floating around in his brain somewhere, they were as difficult to pin down as the woman who had taught them to him.

Cox answered on the first ring. He said, 'The good news is Sven's junketing. He's—'

'I know,' Jacob said. 'What's the bad news?'

'*Courier* city desk called, asked if it was OK to send a feature writer and a photographer over for a Sunday edition interview.'

'You told them you were unavailable?'

'Don't be dense, Jacob. Not with me, with you, of course. It was that new guy, that hotshot from the *Washington Post* Howie hired to be his managing editor when Joe Campbell got sick. I told him *you* were unavailable. I didn't get the feeling he was satisfied.'

'He wasn't.'

'How do you know?'

'Beck put the arm on me for lunch. At lunch he'll put the arm on me for what his m.e. couldn't wangle out of you. What's in Howie's mind is how he delayed breaking the story on that Morganstern kidnapping because we asked him to. Remember?'

'I remember.'

'Do you remember telling him how grateful we were, and that as far as you were concerned he held an IOU he could cash on demand?'

'Yeah.'

'He had that cash-in look in his eye.'

On Cox's desk, Jacob knew, was a souvenir bullet, a .50 calibre slug with his marine regiment number stencilled on it. He had carried it through two campaigns in Vietnam and through three administrations in the Tri-Towns. He thought of it as magic, as a totem for warding off inimical spirits. But it had collateral uses as well. It was ideal for desk tapping during phone conversations, while Cox made up his mind about something, changed his mind about something, or painfully temporized. In this latter mode, the bullet's brisk beat would slow to a dirge-like drag, which could irritate Jacob to the point of madness and was what he heard now.

'There's this other thing I'm remembering,' Cox said. 'It's how Knudsen's real displeased whenever you get ink and that this is a particularly sensitive time for you to get some. But I guess you know that.'

'I guess I do.'

'Yeah, I guess you would.'

Jacob sighed. 'If lightning strikes I'll get hit with this brilliant approach to delaying tactics. But unless that happens Howie gets his quid pro quo—one, because he has it coming. And two, because there's no way we won't need him again. As for Knudsen, what can I tell you, Captain? With the help of God and two policemen, maybe I'll survive.'

'How would you rate your chances?'

'Of surviving?'

'Of lightning striking.'

Jacob kept silent and after a while Cox said, 'Shit,' and disconnected.

Jacob glanced at the message from Commissioner McCracken and had just decided to misplace it in the wastepaper basket when the phone rang. The woman's voice was as billed, husky and deep. Grating, Jacob thought at first, and then almost instantly changed his mind. An OK voice, actually, but not one of those that put in much time trying to make an impression.

'Lieutenant Horowitz?'

He acknowledged it.

'I'm Winifred Cantrell. Is the name familiar to you?'

'Robin's aunt,' he said.

'Yes.' Pause. 'I've been wondering whether you would be interested in speaking with me.'

'Should I be?'

'Well, you see, I'm not at all certain. I heard on the radio this morning that you're looking for Bryant Gilchrist, and I'm convinced that's a mistake.'

'Join the army.'

'Pardon?'

'Never mind.'

'Damn, damn, I feel so idiotic about this. It's not as if I have anything concrete to contribute. I mean, even this one wretched phone call is probably a total waste of time. And yet...'

He waited.

'I couldn't not make it,' she said. Like a distance runner, she blew her breath out heavily, then sucked in another. But when she continued she sounded steadier, as if she had sighted home. 'I suppose what I'm trying to say is I knew Robin better, I think, than anyone. Better, certainly, than she knew herself. And I hate the thought that her killer may get away scot free.'

'Who, in your view, has no chance of being Bry Gilchrist.'

'Yes. I mean no, I don't think that's possible.'

'Could you give me a guess as to who is? Possible, I mean.'

'No.'

'If we got together, would you guess then?'

'No.' But he thought there might have been an instant's hesitation.

'And just to cross the t's and dot the i's, if you knew where Bry was, you wouldn't tell me, right?'

'I wouldn't, no.'

Jacob sighed. 'OK, yeah, I'd like to meet with you. I'm not sure why either. Call it a hunch. Are you in the area?'

'Actually not.'

A sense of significant distances touched Jacob's consciousness, but that hunch was unwelcome and he brushed it off. 'Still, you'll be visiting these parts soon, right? Friends in New York City? Jersey, maybe?'

'I don't have friends anywhere any longer. I seem to have outgrown my need for them. And I hate telephones. I hear myself saying that, and I know you must think I'm an old crank. Or an old fool. Or heaven knows what. I can't imagine why you don't hang up on me.'

'That makes two of us,' Jacob said, but in an unintelligible mutter. Aloud, he said, 'You hate phones, and probably you're not often seen on cars, buses, trains or planes. Am I getting the hang of it?'

'Yes.'

'What are you, under house arrest?'

He heard a sound that might or might not have been a laugh. 'Something like that,' she said.

'So what you're telling me is if we're going to meet I have to come to where you are.'

'Yes.'

'Which isn't around the corner.'

'No.'

'And I'm gathering that you're, like, unsure of what you'll say if I should get there, right?'

'I'll say . . . I'll tell you . . . No. Not really. Lieutenant, you see this whole thing as absurd, and I don't blame you. It's just that for the past week or so I've had . . . this fantasy, that if I talked to you about Robin you'd be skilled enough to find . . . some kind of Rosetta Stone, I suppose. But that's ridiculous, isn't it? And what a far piece to come for such an iffy reward, though of course I'd be eager to put you up for as long as you wanted to stay.'

'How far a piece exactly?'

'Brunswick, Georgia. I'm not at all sure you've heard of it, but it's only three miles from a resort that used to be quite famous.'

'What resort's that?'

'Jekyll Island.'

'Bless you,' Jacob said, not missing a beat, 'that's not so far. I thought you meant far.'

With Miss Cantrell's collaboration he at once set about developing travel plans and honing in on an estimated time of arrival.

'You really and truly will turn up here tomorrow evening, then?' she said wonderingly.

'You like chocolate?'

'Yes.'

'I'll be the one carrying this heart-shaped box.'

Hanging up, he yelled for Mary to cancel his lunch with Howie Beck, who, quid pro quo notwithstanding, would have to forgive a person hell bent on taking the negative out of un-search.

CHAPTER 4

Jekyll Island. A creature-friendly place, Helen thought, the air sweet, the breeze benign, the temperature comfortably in the high forties. She was at her ease on the porch that wrapped around the second floor of the two-storey building of which her room formed the west corner, a pleasantly scratchy blanket wrapped around her toast-warm self.

The building—white, wooden frame, big and solidly constructed—had once been called 'Bachelors' Quarters' and was now unisexed to 'Annexe'. She powered her rocking-chair gently, sleepily, the sun amiable on her back and shoulders. Off to her left was the hotel complex's main building, 'The Clubhouse'—larger, more of a ramble to it, but clearly big brother to a bracketing pair of guest houses. Off to the right, far out on the bay, there was a boat, or ship, something afloat. She sort of watched it.

Soothed by Jekyll, she was experiencing an optimistic stirring, the first of its kind since her departure from the Tri-Towns two days earlier. Already, she had decided she would call Jacob that night, mend fences. Maybe she could even get him to break out, drive down here in the spirit of the-hell-with-everything. In the spirit of—you'd love the air and the water, Jacob dearest, and romping with me on the near-white, near-endless beach.

Well, no, she probably couldn't pull off that kind of miracle, but at least they could reconnect. It felt awful without him. It felt lonely in a way she thought had been banished forever, banished by him and his all-out attack on the self-indulgence of attenuated widowhood.

'Enough of such nonsense,' he had declared, sweeping her up, out, and back into life.

She shook her head, dismayed. To get *that* angry. How foolish. How dangerous. Jacob couldn't help his kind of fidgeting, she knew that. But usually he was good about keeping it in check. And usually she was good about managing it from her end—early defusing through gentle and affectionate teasing.

What had been different? She pulled her coat collar higher and scrunched down into the blanket, in effect hiding from what had been different. The truth was she felt drawn to Bryant and his little-boy-lost quality. The corollary that heated her cheeks was—going to bed wouldn't have killed her.

Her parents, populist radicals—in their sexual politics as well as their social—had raised three daughters to be leary of Puritan hobgoblins. Also, she was a farm girl. Sex, in her witnessing, was too natural and too pervasive to bring on vaporous attacks.

And Jacob, of course, knew that about her. Moreover, ever the shrewd observer, particularly where she was concerned, he had noted the attraction to Bry. But damn him, then, he ought to have known she'd *never*; that her commitment was to their relationship; that the thought of placing it at risk was as much a deterrent as any medieval chastity belt.

Now, despite the sun, she shivered. She rose in her chair, and only the certainty that he would be closeted with Cox at their Wednesday morning briefing session, kept her from seeking a phone there and then. She forced herself back down. She shut her eyes, took a series of deep, purifying breaths, and, having met the Jekyll Island mystique half way, she was at length once more able to relax.

'But you're a big old fool, Jacob Horowitz,' she said, growling into the blanket. 'And if I had you here right now I might kick butt.'

Jekyll Island had been dedicated to relaxing since late in the nineteenth century, a rich man's realized fantasy—restricted, of course. From her lap she lifted the slim volume she'd bought in the hotel gift shop and resumed reading:

To live on an island! Who among us but has felt the fascination of this idea? From the youngster playing his first game of pirates and buried treasure to the oldster who is beginning to weary somewhat of the pressure of his omnipresent fellow men, we all know the lure of the romance which life on an island suggests.

Yet for men of imagination and means the improbable is not always the impossible; and the Jekyll Island Club exists today as the ingenious solution to the difficult problem of finding profound seclusion and congenial companionship in one and the same spot.

That rhapsody to conspicuous consumption had been written by a club member in 1916, and some of the 'men of imagination and means' for whom the improbable turned out not to be impossible were named J. P. Morgan, William Rockefeller, Vincent Astor, and William K. Vanderbilt. Women of imagination and means, Helen noted, need not apply.

At any rate, all the above had bought plots and erected 'cottages' in this off-season Newport. The Clubhouse—impeccably built, generously sized, but surprisingly unpretentious—had been completed in 1886, and by 1889, from January through April, the fat cat programme was in full swing. Whist and bridge by a Clubhouse fireplace; hunting, fishing, bicycling, horseback and buggy-riding for the more vigorous.

Soon enough, facilities for golf and tennis had been provided, including one of America's first indoor courts. Croquet, too, serious croquet—for which Jekyll Island was to become a hotbed. And, the over-privileged being what they were, Helen was willing to add philandering to the list, her money on Jekyll as a hotbed for that as well.

But in 1942, with the war, decline had set in. Now the state of Georgia owned the island and a well-known hostelry chain operated the Clubhouse. Still, the beauty of the place hadn't changed much: some twenty-odd miles of stunning beach, woodlands and marshes. Idyllic Jekyll Island—how predictable of the toffs to want to hang 'Keep Out' signs all over it.

She heard the phone in her room and reluctantly got herself out of the rocker to answer. The caller identified himself as Tom Boswell and sounded unwelcoming.

'I'm godawful tired of being hounded,' he said without much preamble.

'I don't blame you,' she said, soothingly, she hoped.

'I'm tired of police, tired of reporters, tired of all you goddam parasites.'

'Of course you are.'

'Horowitz. That's the name of that Tri-Towns cop who was all over us after Robin got it. Yeah, the ape with a brain. You related to him?'

'His wife.' Adding hurriedly, 'But this isn't police business. I'm a private investigator, working for Bry Gilchrist.'

She half expected the phone to be slammed down, but it was not. What she got instead was a belly laugh. 'Do me a favour,' he said in its wake. 'When you talk to your husband tone down the description a little, OK?'

'OK.'

'Understand you've been here since yesterday?'

'Yes.'

'Well, what's it about? I've got no objection talking to you, you understand, but I've been over the same damn ground a hundred times already, two hundred. What's left to say?'

'I'm not sure.'

'Nothing, that's what.'

'Maybe you're right.'

Upbeat laugh reprised. 'OK, OK, we won't send you home without an honest shot. You want to talk to all of us? I mean Sherry and Jatie as well as me?'

'I'd like to.'

'We were all out on Sam Fletcher's yacht the past couple of days until this morning. He sends it for us when we come down here. He's a Georgia congressman, you know.'

'I didn't.'

'Well, he is. A congressman and a groupie, could you believe?' He sounded both impressed and amused. 'Vera's not here. Did you think she would be?'

'I was hoping.'

'She's not. It's her party, she's picking up the tab for this blast, but she's not here yet and may not make the scene at all. And if that gets you upset, you ought to see what it's doing to Jatie.'

Now the laugh had a marked degree of malice in it, giving Helen a revisionist's pause. Good-natured one minute, malicious the next, the Boswell persona swung pendulum-like, it seemed. All she had known about him going in was the little Bry had told her, Bry typically tight-lipped.

'Where are you now, Mr Boswell?'

'Tom. And what's your first name?'

She told him.

'I'm at the tennis court, the indoor one. And yeah, if you want to talk this would be a good time. Matter of fact, I just finished hitting with Sherry, and she's still here. Want me to hold her for you?'

'No, thanks. I'll catch up with her later.'

'Right. You want to see each of us alone. That's good interviewing technique. Hell, I know that. I watch TV.' The on-again, off-again Rotary Club laugh made a final appearance.

Helen joined in politely.

He cut his off, and when he spoke Helen knew they were back to square one, if, in fact, they had ever left it. 'Could you be wondering why I'm being so all-out cooperative?'

She waited.

'It's because you said the magic word—Bry.'

'You're that fond of him?'

'I want him brought down for what he did to Robin. Everybody knows that. Which means they all expect me to grease the skids. And since I flat out hate and despise doing what everybody expects, I won't.'

'I see.'

'No, you don't. But then nobody else does either. Nobody ever has.'

Helen hung fire, thinking there might be more to come in the way of autobiography, but there wasn't. Instead, after some tuneless whistling, he said, 'How can people stand that murdering son of a bitch?'

'Murdering?'

'You heard me.'

'Whatever happened to presumed innocent?'

'Listen, I'm not trying to argue you into anything. You want to believe in Saint Bry, feel free. After that there's Santa Claus and Tinker Bell.'

'I'm just wondering why you're so convinced.'

'I've got my reasons.'

'Do the police know what they are?'

'Hey, don't Mr and Mrs Cop talk to each other?'

'I mean have you actually told them?'

'Yeah, I told them.'

Though the words could hardly have been more straightforward, there was an odd quality to his voice, as if he had said something enigmatic. Before she could try for elaboration, however, he pushed his own question.

'Helen, old girl, let's cut the bullshit and get down to cases. I mean, there's something important I got to know. And I got to know it right now.'

'What is it?'

'Are you as good-looking as everybody says you are?'

She felt no obligation to reply to that and didn't.

'Everybody says you're a stunner.'

'Who's everybody, Tom?'

'The tour, Helen, the tour. That's who everybody is. Everybody who matters. You with me?'

'Yes.'

'Ten minutes, or I'm gone.' He hung up.

It was red brick, emphatically rectangular, and decidedly squat. Like most of its neighbouring structures, Helen thought, an entirely unremarkable building, except for a certain generic sturdiness. It was as if Jekyll architects and designers had committed themselves wholeheartedly and unanimously to a rigorous guiding principle: let the island provide the æsthetics, we'll build to last. In Helen's view they had got that right.

Though the lights were out, she could observe through the gloom that there was only one court. Empty, she thought at first. She double-checked her watch, affirming that she still had four of her allotted ten. At that moment a ball hurtled by her nose, hit the wall beside her, ricocheted off that, and then off the back of her head. Since by that time the force was fairly well spent it didn't hurt. Had it crunched against her nose, however, it would have hurt a lot.

He was at the net, racket in follow-through position, watching her—like some adolescent, she thought, who had just issued a challenge and was waiting now for the opportunity to yell chicken. Well, he was going to be disappointed. There was a half-empty bucket next to him. She guessed he'd been bending to gather stray balls, which was why she hadn't seen him on entering.

'Sorry about that, Helen, old girl,' Boswell said. 'You should have made some noise.'

'Should I have?'

'Hell, yes. Good reflexes, though. Got that beak out of the way like a pro.'

'Thanks.'

She retrieved the ball.

'Played a bit of sports in your time?' he asked, holding the bucket towards her so she could add to the collection.

'Some. Pitched for my college.'

'Yeah?'

'Yeah,' she said and when only two yards separated them buried the ball in his groin. 'Side-armer.'

He grunted and doubled over. The bucket fell, littering the court with its contents. His racket was leaning against the net, and she took charge of it lest vengeance enter his thoughts once the pain subsided.

That did not happen right away.

When it did sufficiently to allow for other considerations he turned from her and undid his waistband. The next interval was devoted to survey and inventory. At length, he refastened himself. Still bent, he took an extra minute or two to work on his breathing. But when finally he got himself erect he managed to surprise her.

'One for your side,' he said mildly. 'I'll be ready next time.'

'No, you won't.'

His mouth twitched, but he was not yet in shape for full out amusement, though the deep breath he took now seemed almost normal.

'Tough broad, aren't you?'

'It goes like this. Never give a jerk an even break. But I'm finished if you are.'

She held out her hand, and he took it.

'My mom was a tough broad,' he said. 'Maybe that's why I've always been drawn to them.'

'Have you been?'

He sprinted away from her, twenty feet or so, then back. 'Feels OK,' he said. 'Though I'll probably piss blood.'

'Not for long,' she said phlegmatically.

He grinned. 'And Vera, too. She's another tough broad.'

'World class, from what I hear.'

He looked at her. 'Somehow I get the feeling you've been listening to people with a grudge. You been listening to Gilchrist?'

'Bry has a grudge against Vera?'

'He's got grudges against almost everybody.'

'Tell me about the one against you.'

His gestures conveyed locked lips and a discarded key.

'I thought I was supposed to get this honest shot,' she said.

'Two things I learned from my dear dead pappy, who beyond that wasn't worth shit to me. One, play tennis well enough, and you won't have to work for a living. Two, keep your business to yourself and never, *ever* get involved.'

'I think that might be three,' Helen said.
'Consider you just got a bonus.'
'All right, if you won't talk about you, tell me about Vera. What's Bry's grudge against her?'
'Listen, there's this whole beggar army wanting something from Vera. And whoever don't get it usually winds up with a grudge.'
'Bry wants something from Vera?'
He shrugged.
'I don't know, Tom. It all sounds pretty vague to me.'
'If that's what you think, then that's what you think.'
'What I think is you dislike Bry so much you'll say anything about him, anything incriminating that might have even a slim chance of being believed. I think you'd *love* to grease the skids. You just don't want to be seen doing it.'
'Interview over. So long. Nice knowing you.' He took a step away but then surprised her once more by coming back. 'Hey, you behave yourself, understand? You're only a private cop. That means I don't owe you a goddam minute more than I want to give. OK?'
'OK.'
He nodded. 'All right, so be polite.'
'Is it impolite to go down the list of what the beggar army wants from Vera?'
Hesitantly: 'Maybe not.'
'Starting with you, I mean.'
For a moment she thought he'd take her to task again, but he didn't. He smiled. 'You're a pistol, aren't you? All right, but the fact is, I'm here because she asked me to come. And she asked me to come because she can't stand being alone. The thing about Vera is she won't even go to the toilet alone if she can help it.'
He was silent a moment then, inwardly debating, after which his expression underwent a curious change, a subtle heightening. It was as if—having glimpsed a window of opportunity—his mental set had got up on its toes. But the clue to it all was not immediately apparent. He said, 'And, yeah, since you ask, I want something from her, too.'

'Which is?'

'A job. I want to be her coach. I need that job because I happen to be flat broke. Also, I can do it a lot better than that Argentine headcase—Ramirez, I mean. Why am I telling you this? Because you just never know where your next good angel's coming from. You might just be there at the tactical moment.'

'Be where?'

'I don't know. Wherever Vera is, whispering the right word in her shell-like ear.'

The pieces had fallen into place. She smiled. 'Me, your good angel? You honestly think I might qualify?'

'Sure. There's nothing like a tennis ball in the crotch to bring people closer together.' He beetled his brows at her and did some Groucho stuff with a mimed cigar.

He was quite a package, she thought. All those freckles and sandy hair, but with that lurking hard-guy cynicism to keep smart girls from getting bored. And what *was* he up to? Was he out to bury Bry because—as he implied—of an abstract desire to see justice served? Or was the spur more basic, something as time-honoured as a guilty man's need to shift suspicion. The Boswell motive ranked up there with the best: jealousy. The Boswell opportunity? His alibi was as negligible and as open to scepticism as anyone's.

'I thought you were Hattie Lockridge's coach,' she said.

'Scratch that. Hattie's gone back to Mama, and Mama's got her own plans about coaching. They don't include me.'

'Let's see now if I'm getting this straight. You want to be Vera's coach, but Jatie already is, so I suppose I can figure out what Jatie wants from Vera.'

He nodded. 'Yeah. He wants her to boot my ass out of here. But the fact is, if she did, it wouldn't cause a real lot of change in his young life.'

'What does that mean?'

'It means what it goddam means.'

'I see.' And actually she thought she did.

He snatched the racket from her hand, grabbed a ball from the bucket and smashed it off the nearest wall. Then, quite gently, he handed the racket back to her. 'It means, dammit, that nothing's forever. And I don't want to talk about it any more.'

'OK, what does Sherry want from Vera?'

'God, you don't even slow down.'

She waited.

'Beats me,' he said. 'If you know Sherry at all you know she marches to her own drummer.'

'Could it have something to do with you?'

'How?'

Helen had no idea, but she had the sense of a conversation that might still produce a nugget or two if she could keep it going long enough. Borrowing from that master of improvisation, her husband, whose operating principle had always been, if you shake 'em up you might shake it loose, she said, 'Something to do with your ending Robin's marriage?'

'That's crap.'

'Are you telling me—'

'What I'm telling you is friggin' Bry Gilchrist didn't find me in bed with his wife no matter how many friggin' times he says he did. She was my meal ticket, and I couldn't afford to risk that by stepping out of line. OK, I liked her. I wasn't dippy about her the way he was, but I did like her. And if she'd offered I probably would have taken her up. But she didn't. Period. The end.'

'Never?'

'No.'

'Not even that once?'

'You heard me.'

'Who did take her up?'

'Whoever did, that's his business.'

'But someone did.'

'Jesus, is it your impression Robin was the Virgin Mary?'

He looked at her, not angrily, she thought, but speculatively. Once again he was about to put her to some kind of test, she decided, a variation on the tennis-ball-to-the-nose trial. And if somehow she passed that then there'd be a third. And a fourth. She guessed he went through life that way—with little-boy tests in aid of little-boy judgements.

He grinned at her. 'You believe me?'

'Maybe.'

'Not that I give a shit, really. You can believe what you goddam please. To me it's just a question of how smart you are.'

They were silent then, studying each other detachedly, the way people do who find each other interesting but not altogether likeable.

'If you want to, you can take your shower now,' a voice behind Helen said. 'I'll entertain Mrs Horowitz.'

Boswell reacted with the kind of enthusiasm that suggested to Helen he'd had enough of her. Even before the speech was finished his belongings were gathered, and he was into his exit. Only something in the nature of a police barrier could have stopped him, Helen thought.

Turning, she saw an attractive young woman in a trench coat over sweats just coming through a door labelled 'Women's Lockers'. She recognized her instantly.

Sherry nodded. 'In photographs we don't look that much alike. In real life we do—did.' Changing tenses, Helen noted, but not expressions. 'I recognized you, too, you know. Saw your picture on your husband's desk. He's not here with you?'

'No. As I told—'

'Yes, I know what you told Tom. Just wanted to make sure. If you don't mind my saying so, your husband scares me. Does he scare everyone?'

'Everyone he finds it useful to scare. Which usually means everyone he talks to during an investigation. He'd hate it if he heard me saying that. He'd call it giving away professional secrets.'

'He doesn't scare you, I bet.'

'Actually, he does. I just never let on.'

Sherry laughed, came forward, and took Helen's hand, leading her to one of the sideline chairs. 'Look at this place,' she said when they were seated. 'Sixty years old, and it'll last forever. I love playing here. It feels so . . . Gatsbyish. Twenty-five thousand got it all built. Imagine.' She broke off, glanced at the floor for a moment and then said, 'I'm gushing. I think that's because I'm tremendously relieved.'

'About what?'

'About you. I didn't know what to expect, you see. But now I can understand why Bry has such perfect confidence in you. You'll help him. I know you will.'

Helen looked at her speculatively. 'My guess is I'm talking to someone who could point me to where he is.'

Sherry took a moment. 'If I say yes now, and you tell the police I'll say you're a liar.'

'I won't tell the police.'

'You won't? Not even your husband?'

'I'll try again to convince Bry that if he's smart he'll turn himself in, but I won't rat on him. No, not even to Jacob.'

'I think I believe you.'

'Good.'

'You can forget about him turning himself in, though.'

'Why?'

'Because he's absolutely determined not to, at least not while things are the way they are now. He thinks the case against him is very strong. That's why he ran in the first place. If he turns himself in he's certain he'll go to gaol. Could you promise he won't?'

'Promise? No.'

'Well, that terrifies him, the thought of being locked up. You should see. He gets white and shivery. He . . . It goes back to what happened to him as a child, of course.'

'What was that?'

'You don't know?'

'Bry always makes like a clam when it comes to his so-called formative years. With me, that is.'

'Yes. He would. I think that's because he . . .'

'What?'

'Promise you won't take this the wrong way.'

'Promises are not my favourite thing,' Helen said. Somehow—she couldn't pinpoint it—she was beginning to feel patronized. And she was beginning not to like it.

'You *are* annoyed,' Sherry said. 'And there's no reason to be.'

Helen collected herself. 'You're right. Sorry. Fire when ready.'

'You're sure you won't mind?'

'I *promise*.'

Sherry smiled faintly. 'It's just that some people don't have as much tolerance for weakness as others. I don't mean that to be critical. Please don't misunderstand me. It's just that some people are so strong and self-sufficient themselves that they lack . . . Oh, this is all coming out wrong. I meant only that he always wanted you to approve of him.'

'Where do I come off approving or disapproving? I'm just an ordinary sinner like the rest of us.'

'Bry doesn't think so.'

'Bry's cock-eyed. I've had my pathetic times, too, for God's sake.'

She had an absurd urge to cite cases but squelched it as pointless. They—Bry and his spokesperson—had reinvented her larger than life, and the facts of the matter were not likely to cause a shrinking.

Sherry smiled her tolerance at Helen's outburst. It was a sweet and sympathetic smile, immutable as marble.

Sighing inwardly, Helen looked for a way to start over. 'Anyway, I sometimes get the feeling Bry was born thirty-something,' she said. 'But he wasn't, was he?'

'Oh no.'

'So tell me.'

Sherry flamed up. 'It was his father, his drunken sot of a father who used to shut him up in closets for hours, for whole afternoons. God, the wickedness of that.'

Helen studied her. For a moment Sherry turned away, as if in self-defence. But then her glance came up to meet Helen's directly. 'We're lovers,' she said. Adding, 'You don't approve, do you?'

'Again approve. Get it straight, please, once and for all. I'm not in the approving business. Or the disapproving business. Never was. The only thing that matters to me is whether or not you've complicated my life. And I think you have.'

'Why?'

'Just a hunch. Are you going to tell me where Bry is?'

'He'll phone you.'

'No more phone calls. I want to meet with him, eyeball to eyeball. It's time.'

'Maybe. Maybe not yet.'

'I could swear I heard the words perfect confidence only a moment ago.'

Sherry kept silent.

'Hey,' Helen said softly. 'What you and Bry do, you and Bry do. You're both consenting adults.'

'Yes, you say that, but I saw something different in your face. Big letters: HER SISTER'S HUSBAND. Well, that was a travesty. Craziness to begin with, craziness all the way through.' She reached out and touched the back of Helen's hand. 'Think about us, I mean really think about us. And then tell me I'm not better for him than Robin ever was.'

'Much better.'

'You mean that?'

'For what it's worth, but—'

'I know,' Sherry said. 'You're not in the approving business.' Wetness glistened, and she brushed at her eyes impatiently. 'Stupid, isn't it? I hate crying in front of strangers. It used to be only Robin could make me cry. These days almost anybody can. I don't know what's wrong with me.'

'Strain. Don't worry about it.'

'I'll tell him what you said. About meeting. And then it's up to him, of course.'

'OK.'

She stared at Helen. 'Promise you won't betray him. Please promise.'

'Oh, for God's sake.'

'*Please*. He admires you so much. And he's drowning, he really is. He's trying to be brave, but you can see how close he is to coming apart. You can see how alone he thinks he is, and how it's depressing him. And I feel so awful and so helpless. But you're not. You've got the strength to—'

Helen held up both hands. 'Enough!'

Sherry broke off.

'Do you see anything hidden here? Wands or anything?'

'No.'

'The point is, that if Bry does manage to stay out of the slammer it won't be magic that does it. It'll be because someone else goes in his place, OK? And as far as yours truly is concerned, that's a process that gets under way with some fairly rotten questions. Or at least one rotten question.'

'He'll answer—'

'Right now I'm talking about you.'

'Me?'

Helen hesitated, but then having decided it was one of those things that simply had to be faced and got out of the way, said, expressionlessly, 'Did you kill your sister?'

Sherry laughed. It died quickly. 'You're serious?'

'You've spent the last ten minutes giving yourself one hell of a motive. Where *did* you go after Robin's match with Hattie?'

'To the movies. I told your husband that.'

'I remember now. Alone.'

'Yes.'

'Also absolutely unobserved. What are you, a ghost?'

'Please don't use that tone. It's your husband's tone, and I need more than that from you. I loved Robin. She could drive me wild, of course she could, but I really and truly loved her. Please say you believe that.'

In fact, Helen believed it wholeheartedly. Earlier in the day, while rocking, dozing, and generally vegetating, an insight had managed to slice through torpor. On the whole, it was of an unwelcome nature, since as far as she could see, it did little but blur what had already been murky enough. Still, there it was, and she did not doubt its validity.

'The deal is *whoever* murdered your sister loved her. What do you think about that?'

Sherry was furious—eyes smouldering, fists white-knuckled.

'Hey, look at you,' Helen said softly.

'Sometimes . . .'

'Sometimes what?'

'I just think people can be so . . . evil.'

'Who?'

She stared at Helen for a moment. Then she shook her head as if to clear it. Her hand was at her mouth, forestalling further breakthroughs.

'Talk to me,' Helen said.

'No. You're tricky. I say things I don't mean to.'

'Listen, love and hate got mixed up in someone. Result: explosion. That's how it happened. That's how your sister got killed. I need to know who you're thinking of. Come on, Sherry, you *have* to talk to me. Boswell? Jatie? Vera?'

Bingo! Sherry's eyes had widened.

'Vera?'

She turned away, but Helen moved quickly to front her. 'Why Vera?'

'Because she—' But then she broke off. 'No. That's enough. I won't say anything more, and you can't make me.'

And studying her, Helen knew she wouldn't be able to. And, in the same moment, knew that she'd misinterpreted Sherry, that she had taken Sherry as Sherry wanted her to and as a result had underestimated her. Tabby cat only on the surface. Beneath that, a lioness with a cub to protect. But the claws were being sheathed for now.

'I'm sorry,' Sherry said. 'That was unforgivable of me, sounding off that way, God, just like I was Madam Defarge. I wonder what you think of me.'

'I think you meant what you said.'

'Oh, please. Why would Vera do anything to hurt Robin?'

'You tell me.'

'She wouldn't have. Vera loved Robin, adored her. Oh yes, there's your theory to consider. But that's all that is, isn't it, just a theory?'

'OK.'

'Besides, we all know where Vera was when Robin was murdered. Could anyone have a better alibi?'

They were both silent a moment. Then Helen said, 'A terrific alibi. Solid as they come. But it's fascinating how many people seem unconvinced by it. Are you one of them? I mean, is that why you're here?'

'Of course not.'

'Of course not,' Helen said.

'I'm here because Vera's an old friend, and she invited me. Why on earth would you think anything else?'

Helen looked at her. 'I have a piece of advice for you,' she said.

'What?'

'Don't do anything stupid.'

Sherry's head came up sharply, eyes glinting. 'I don't know what you're talking about. For the last few minutes, you've been saying such odd things. You really have. It really makes me wonder how wise we'd be to trust you.'

Helen smiled tightly. 'Who else have you got?'

They saw Tom Boswell crossing the court. Hair still damp from his shower and combed straight back from his freckled forehead, he looked younger than his thirty-four years, and blatantly All-American. He also looked as if he'd just had good news. In a moment he shared it.

'Princess Vera is among us,' he told Sherry. 'Jatie just called. She's checking in right now, and we ought to go along and be a reception committee. You know how she likes a fuss.' He turned to Helen. 'Sherry'll take a raincheck, OK?'

'Why can't she come too?' Sherry asked surprisingly.

'No reason.' But it was clear to Helen that it would have pleased him to be able to think of one.

He never had the chance. Every inch the princess in a sumptuous white leather coat, open to reveal an outrageously sequined pantsuit, red as blood, Vera blew in on them, Jatie in her wake.

Sherry was thoroughly hugged, pressed so close Helen couldn't tell if she liked it or not.

'Little sister,' Vera said enthusiastically, though her eyes were fixed on Helen. 'How glorious to be with you again. Did you think I'd fallen off the face of the earth?' She pushed Sherry slightly away and really looked at her for the first time. She tapped her cheek reprovingly. 'A little pale, Sistersky. We shall have to bake you in the sun. Thomas, you of course are blooming. You are always blooming.' Swinging around to Helen, she held out her hand. 'Welcome, foreign emissary.'

'Thank you,' Helen said. 'I'm—'

'I know who you are, my dear. Why else would I have hurried down here at breakneck speed, not even pausing for the pee I urgently need. Curiosity, of course. Intense, feverish curiosity.'

'Oh?'

'But certainly.' Sigh. 'I abandon hope.'

'Do you? What kind, specifically?'

Dazzling smile. 'That your Jacob might be a husband I could steal.' She patted Helen's hand. 'You are lovely, my dear. Well, perhaps lovely is the wrong word. You are . . . redoubtable.'

'I wouldn't mind your going back to lovely,' Helen said.

Vera studied her. 'What's more, I think I like you. Do you play tennis?'

'Not what you mean by tennis.'

'I mean, can you get the ball back with reasonable consistency?'

'Yes.'

'Good. You will take Jatie's place in our foursome. Jatie, say goodbye to us. Then go and pack your bags. I came here to have a grand time, to relax. I simply cannot do that with you glowering at me.'

They all turned to look at him. For a moment he said nothing. His face had gone pale, but as they watched, it reddened. 'Bitch,' he said.

She eyed him calmly. 'If you speak again, Jatie, our separation may become permanent.'

He took a step forward, but so did Boswell, interposing himself.

'Oh, what a true bitch you really are,' Jatie said. 'I have known this was coming, of course. I could see how much I had begun to bore you, how you could not stand the sight of me or the sound of my voice, how you could not even bear to be in the same room with me.'

His mouth worked silently, shaping and reshaping itself for invective, but since words eluded him, the effect was bizarre—a guppy in a tantrum. In desperation, he spat at her, or rather towards her, clearly intending to miss, which he did.

'*That* for your charade. You think I don't know I have already been replaced?'

'You haven't been, but what a splendid idea,' Vera said. She turned to Boswell. 'I want to beat Hattie in every Grand Slam we play. Most of all I want to crush her in the US Open. Can you help me do these things?'

He nodded.

'Good. You are my coach.' Back to Jatie. 'Within the next few days I'll send you a cheque.'

'Bitch! You think you've heard the last of Jatie Ramirez? You're wrong. You could not be more wrong.' He wheeled into an exit, but after a step or two turned again. 'Slut! Whore!' He paused. 'Dyke!' It came out in a sort of whispered shout, after which he spat and missed and left.

Helen shot a quick glance at Vera but saw no indication that she felt bruised in any way.

'Lovers' partings,' Vera said. 'Often they are not very edifying.' Suddenly she called out, 'Jatie, it will be a particularly handsome cheque.'

'But he was gone by then.

'I probably should have done that differently,' she said, sighing. Her mouth curved downward. Then: 'Oh God, I simply must have my pee.'

Shrugging out of her coat, she tossed it to Boswell and ran, long-strided and graceful, for the appropriate door.

Boswell looked at Helen, smiled, and then clicked his heels in a bleak and cynical bow.

CHAPTER 5

No spring chicken, that house, a hundred if it was a day, Jacob decided. But pretty. White clapboard with green shutters freshly painted. Before it, a tiny lawn immaculately kept. Shaped oddly though, slightly wider in front than in back, a pie wedge of a house. Still, it *was* pretty. And as the only wooden house of the seven on its tree-lined block, it certainly stood out from its neighbours. Jacob guessed its owner might, too. He knocked.

Win Cantrell took a few moments to answer. In fact, he heard her before he saw her, and when he did see her he realized that what he'd heard had been her cane tapping.

'Lieutenant Horowitz?'

'That's right.'

'Come in, please. I told Mary Alice there was someone at the door, but she paid no attention to me. She never does. I sometimes think she's as deaf as I am blind.' She turned and shouted, 'Mary Alice, you come out here and take the Lieutenant's bag. I told you there was someone at the door.'

'You did not. You told me you thought it was time we were hearing his knock.'

'I don't have a bag,' Jacob said.

But Miss Cantrell had clumped away from him. She was a tall, slender woman of sixty or so, who had kept her figure. He thought she must have been beautiful once. Her hair, in a tight bun, was smooth and white against olive skin, nose and mouth perfectly shaped. She wore dark glasses so that Jacob couldn't see her eyes, but his guess was they were brown and large. Brown and large would have matched the rest of what was in her face. She wore a long, black skirt, a beige cardigan sweater, unbuttoned, over a white blouse and bedroom slippers. She looked as if she cared about being clean and being covered, but that was it as far as clothes were concerned.

Mary Alice had now made an appearance. She was black, in her early forties. Very large, though not fat, the looming bulk of a one-time shot-putter, Jacob thought. But her smile was gentle. She nodded at Jacob approvingly—one mountain appreciative of another—took the heart-shaped box of candy he proffered, then ducked back into the kitchen.

He followed Miss Cantrell into her living-room, which was furnished much as she was dressed—clean and comfortable. No frills. Not cheery, not gloomy either.

She motioned him to a seat on the sofa, and he took it. Without much wasted motion she found the rocker across the room and took that. She rocked briskly for a moment, collecting herself, Jacob thought, and waited.

'I wish I knew what you look like,' she said suddenly. 'That's the thing I miss most, you know. Not having that head start about people. You're a big man, aren't you. You make sounds as if you were. Over six feet?'

'Yes.'

'Well over, I'd guess. And you weigh what? About two hundred and thirty?'

'In the neighbourhood.'

She smiled. 'On second thought, maybe a more crowded neighbourhood?'

'About two hundred and fifty-five,' he admitted.

'Hmmm. You *are* big. But not fat, I imagine. Like Mary Alice. She's big but not an ounce of fat on her. You should have seen her on the basketball court. People were afraid of her. I wonder if they are of you.'

'I have a kind face,' he said.

'Do you? Perhaps you wouldn't mind bringing it over here.'

Her fingers were long and graceful, and as they traced his planes and hollows, feathery light. The process took about a minute. She signalled its completion by tapping his cheek gently. 'Now we know each other a bit, don't we? I mean, you learned a little something about me, too.'

'I have this feeling that you're a very clever lady,' he said.

'You're quite right. I am clever. It's part of what made me such an extraordinary teacher. Not just my fifth graders, I meant Robin, too. Robin would not have become the champion she was if it weren't for me. She would never acknowledge that, of course, but it's true. Sherry knows it's true. So does Mary Alice.'

'So did Robin,' Jacob said.

Miss Cantrell kept silent, but he had seen her stiffen. Now she leaned forward. 'Lieutenant, I never have been the kind of southern woman who's comfortable with gallantry. I know very well how Robin felt about me. Nor do I blame her. To her I was a stepmother right out of Hans Christian Andersen. I made mistakes with her, mistakes I never made with Sherry, or any other child for that matter. Discipline can seem much like cruelty to a child if love isn't there to go hand in hand. I felt the love, but somehow I could not communicate it. Sherry once said it was as if two different women lived inside me—her aunt and Robin's. At any rate, it would not be a simple matter to persuade me now that Robin had seen into my heart.'

'She told Bry she did. He told me.'

'What does that mean?'

'She said she'd never been the most talented player on the tour, but that she won on toughness. She told Bry you made her tough, that it had been your goal.'

He saw her take a deep breath and then let it out slowly. After a moment she said, 'Well, thank you for that.'

He kept silent.

'Thank you very much.'

Her hand started towards her glasses, perhaps to her eyes, but she drew it back sharply, the kind of iron gesture he thought was characteristic of her now. He wondered if it had always been. He wondered if she had permitted herself to cry on hearing of Robin's death. He thought not. And then again, bedrooms are havens. Secrets can be kept there.

'How long has it been since you could see?' he asked.

'Five years. That is, five years since I've been totally blind. Seven years since I could see decently. It's a disease, and in another year—two at the outermost—it will kill me, and that's all I intend to say about it. You're not going to spend the night?'

'I can't.'

'But you will stay to dinner?'

'Yes.'

She smiled. 'Good. And how fortunate for you. We're having salmon in one of Mary Alice's special sauces. She's a superb cook, you know. Well, how could you? Oh God, I'm suddenly quite nervous. I wasn't a moment ago, but I am now. Is it you?'

'Not really. That is, I don't think so.'

'Well, what is it?'

'I think you're not happy about what you have to tell me.'

She was silent a long moment. Then she said, 'I almost called you back and told you not to come. But Mary Alice wouldn't let me. She said I'd either talk to you or fret myself to a frazzle, and that my kind of fretting was beyond anything she could stand.' She raised her voice a bit so it could be heard in the kitchen. 'And I always listen to Mary Alice.'

A derisive laugh issued out in response. While it was still in the air Mary Alice appeared with a tray. Two mugs of coffee were on it, and a plate of biscuits. She gave one of the mugs to Miss Cantrell.

'You look like you're fixin' to faint from hunger,' she said to Jacob. 'These'll tide you till dinner. Coffee might be a mite powerful.'

He sipped. 'Just right.' It was; strong and restorative after his long drive.

'Try a biscuit,' Miss Cantrell said. 'Oatmeal and raisin. Mary Alice is famous for her oatmeal biscuits.'

The women watched as intently as if he were a spectator sport.

'Does he like it?' Miss Cantrell asked.

'I believe he does, sure enough,' Mary Alice said.

'Delicious,' Jacob said.

Both women registered relief and pleasure.

'I'd have given you hard liquor,' Mary Alice said, 'but she won't allow any in the house.'

'Mary Alice nips,' Miss Cantrell said.

'I most certainly do not,' she said indignantly, starting back to the kitchen. But at the door she stopped, looked back at Jacob and with a sudden flash of white teeth, said, 'I was never any kind of mincing, namby-pamby nipper. Not my style, no way. In my time I was what you'd call a flat out, go-for-it guzzler.'

'Well, she was,' Miss Cantrell said when the door had closed behind her. 'Mary Alice is an alcoholic. A long, long time ago she was the smartest fifth-grader I ever had. Went on to become a mathematician, brilliant. But she drank herself out of positions at three universities. She's been sober now for two years. I keep telling her she's ready to go back into the world. She keeps telling me the world's no fitting place for a sane woman to go back to. Actually she won't go anywhere until I die, you understand. Which means I'm her gaoler, in effect.'

Jacob started to speak, but she held up her hand to cut him off.

'I hate that, of course,' she said. 'But dear God, what would I do without her?'

'I've seen thousands of gaolbirds,' Jacob said. 'She doesn't look like any of them.'

Suddenly she glanced up at the ceiling as if something

there had caught her attention, or as if not being able to see what Jacob could, she could see what he couldn't.

'Are you a man who's easily shocked? My guess is you're not.'

'My guess is you're right.'

She nodded. 'There is a certain evenness in your inflection that suggests evenness of disposition. One could describe it as—'

'A monotone,' he said. 'In grade school they would never let me sing.'

'Did you want to?'

'Yeah. I think I probably memorized more lyrics than any kid in the Philadelphia school system, for all the good it ever did me.'

She laughed.

Putting his mug down on the table next to him, he leaned forward. 'Miss Cantrell,' he said, 'I'm not easily shocked, nor am I easily put off. What I am is a cop chasing down information. But I won't mistreat it, if you know what I mean.'

'I think so.'

'I mean no one's going to get railroaded.'

She sighed, then took a deep breath. 'It's Vera Menchicov I want to talk about, God forgive me.'

'I'm listening,' Jacob said.

CHAPTER 6

Climbing the stairs to her second-floor room, Helen thought about how strained an affair dinner had been. Jatie had hovered over it, ghostlike, a haunt not banishable by the magnum of champagne Vera had ordered to 'drive off whatever damn dybbuks there were'. Sherry had left early, claiming a headache. Shortly thereafter—seemingly of one accord—Tom, Vera, and Helen herself had stood from the table, muttered formulaic phrases at each other, and drifted apart.

Helen had wandered down to the pier. The night, bright with stars and full moon, was reflected in the waters of the bay. Beautiful, she thought, but it was the kind of beauty that put an edge on simple loneliness. She evoked Jacob, who refused to linger.

But where on earth was he? She had phoned—once, twice, three times. No answer. She bit her lip. What if their quarrel froze somehow, becoming, through perversity, part of a new status quo, so that . . . *ridiculous*! They were who they were, for heaven's sake, not some jerry-built ersatz couple to cave in at a fly's worth of pressure. They had a history, a seamlessness crafted by effort, skill and caring.

But for a moment her stomach had gone empty, and the shiver that caused her to haul up her collar had had nothing to do with any sudden gust, for there was none. She had then evoked the events of the day, activating her mind as a way of bemusing it.

'Dyke,' Jatie had said. What to make of that? Was he to be taken literally? She tried to think of Vera in those terms and found it all but impossible. But that didn't mean it couldn't be true. Or at least have truth in it.

She had managed to catch up with Jatie for just a minute before he left, not that it gained her much.

'It is no business of yours, none.' The thin, broody face was distant. Something out of kilter in it, she thought, so that for a moment it seemed to her he might not even know who she was. In the next moment she learned that was wrong. 'Jatie Ramirez needs no peeper woman poking into his affairs. Now get out of my way before I break your fucking head.'

And bye-bye Jatie.

It was at this point that the night had turned cold, far less conducive to strolling than it had been only fifteen minutes earlier. Then there had been couples, four or five of them, populating the paths in front of the Clubhouse. Now she was alone. She shivered again. Unfriendly spirits stirred in the rising wind, rendering her sullen and sorry for herself, but stoical despite this. Let the bad times roll, she told herself grimly, heading for her room.

Having turned the key in the lock, she grew suddenly alert. Some extra sense had kicked into operation, and she knew, beyond question, she wasn't alone.

She stepped back, reopened her purse, and withdrew a tiny revolver, her travellin'-light .22.

Moonlight seeping into the room revealed no one. She double-checked to be sure, while using that time to prepare for what she was going to do next.

Her heart was beating fast but not too fast. Her hand was steady. As softly as she could, then, she crossed to the bathroom, gathered herself, and jerked hard at the door with her left hand, weapon ready in the other.

But that room was also empty.

'You're dead three times already,' a voice said. It came from the porch, the door to which was now slid back. She dropped gun and purse and ran into Jacob's arms. These remained unwelcoming for several seconds before wrapping themselves around her tightly enough to imperil ribs.

Her eyes were shut, but she knew his weren't. 'Stop that,' she said.

'What?'

'Looking at me that way. It makes me shy.'

'What a big, gorgeous woman you are.'

'I've got stretch marks.'

'So?'

'It makes me shy to think of you studying them.'

'I wasn't studying your stretch marks. You want me to study your stretch marks? Say so, and maybe after a while I'll get around to them.'

'No.'

'No what?'

'Forget about my stretch marks. What I want is for you to hold me and explain to me in decent detail how and why you're here. God, Jacob, I've spent practically this whole day thinking about you and missing you. And now, just like that, you're here. How?'

'Merlin's my name, magic's my game.'

A gentle though suggestive pull on the hair of his chest. 'OK, OK, I'll talk.'

She released him, but he noted clawed fingers kept in readiness. 'First,' she said, 'I want to know how you got into the room.'

'I asked for you at the desk, flashed my badge, and told them you were a suspect in a murder case.'

'Honest to God?'

'No.'

'You sneaked up and picked the lock is what you did.'

He nodded. 'Piece of cake. All these pre-nineteen-twenty locks are.'

'Go on.'

He got up on an elbow and grinned. 'Aren't you going to ask if I'm hungry? I mean, what kind of a wife doesn't ask a question like that. All those miles? This late at night? You should be ashamed, Helen Horowitz.'

'Are you hungry?'

'No. I stopped for dinner.'

'Am I supposed to ask where?'

'Around the corner.'

'Jacob, I could do things to things of yours ... around the corner *where?*'

'Win Cantrell's,' he said. 'She lives in Brunswick.'

She stared at him.

'Brunswick? Across the causeway? Four, five miles? That Brunswick. You didn't know?'

'No. How did you?'

Elaborate, temper-trying yawn. 'Just good police work,' he said. 'Some of us are born to it.'

But then, judging that she might be getting ready to exploit the vulnerability she had called to his attention, he delayed no further in telling her of Win Cantrell's phone call, of their meeting, and, finally, of what had resulted from that.

Helen listened intently. When Jacob had finished, she lay quiet in his arms, thinking. He let the silence gather, thinking for his own part only how glad he was to be with her, their anger gone, their companionable ease back in place. He watched the gentle rise and fall of her bosom and placed his head there.

'Do you believe her?'

'I don't think Win Cantrell knows how to lie,' he said.

'Tell me again. I mean that part about how she caught them. God, how awful that must have been.'

'*In flagrante*,' Jacob said. 'One of those freakish accidents that does make you wonder sometimes. It's 'eighty-one, Vera's first Wimbledon. Aunt Win and Sister Sherry go shopping. Five, ten minutes, and in a sudden drenching downpour they scurry back to the hotel. They decide to collect Robin and take her to tea. Sherry unlocks the door to the room she shares with Robin, and there's her sibling in a tanglement, naked and unashamed.'

'Wow!'

'Yeah.'

'You'd think they'd have been more careful. Why that room? Why not Vera's?'

'But that's the essence of them, isn't it?'

'What is?'

'That Robin was—and Vera is—too flamboyant to take pains. Carelessness, it's the key to their charm.'

'Hmmm.'

'At any rate, Sherry slams the door shut and runs, but, after a brief pause to gather courage, Win knocks, goes in. What does she say to the guilty pair? She tells them they're begging for trouble, and that if they've got a brain between them they'll cease and desist. When they indicate no way, that they couldn't if they wanted to, she delivers this big-time lecture on the value of discretion. They promise to give that a try. Thanking them for small favours, she tells them she'll meet them in the tea-room in fifteen minutes.'

'I like Aunt Win. She doesn't self-destruct.'

'A Cucumber Kate, my grandpa would have called her.

I mean, she's too much the traditionalist to feel terrific about the Vera/Robin kind of relationship but note the lack of wasted breath. And the fact is she can still admire Vera a lot, for her style, her independent spirit, her refusal to be anyone's Vera but her own, stuff like that. On the other hand, Win's a firm believer in accepting responsibility for one's own acts. Translation: if Vera killed Robin she has to pay for it.'

'*Does* Win think Vera killed Robin?'

Jacob was silent a long moment. Then: 'What she thinks is that Bry couldn't possibly murder anyone, but that Vera, when her blood's up, could. Now she didn't exactly say that, not in so many words, but that's what she thinks.'

Helen toyed with Jacob's chest hair, wrapping tendrils of it around her fingers hard enough to hurt. He slapped her hand away. In a moment, however, unthinkingly, she was back at work. For reasons of his own, he decided not to complain.

'Sherry Cantrell gives me the willies,' she said at length, a change of subject that wasn't much of one, he soon discovered. 'There's this doom feeling I have about her, as if she's trying to nerve herself to some major act—should she, shouldn't she? Like Hamlet.'

Jacob considered. He pictured her: small face, large eyes, pale, intense, always painstakingly turned out and said, 'Maybe.'

'I've been thinking,' Helen said, 'that if I were Vera I'd be grateful for a warning.'

'So warn her.'

'No, you warn her, Jacob. She'd be ever so much more appreciative.' She looked at him. 'Do *you* admire Vera for her independent spirit and refusal to be anyone else's Vera but her own?'

'Why do you ask?' he asked uneasily.

'She admires you, you know.'

'Does she?'

'Oh yes. I get the feeling she could eat you right up. I

mean, she's clearly not one of those women whose sexual preferences are strictly defined, is she?'

'I guess not.'

'So what I want to know, Jacob, is if in addition to her independent spirit, you also admire her ass?' Where she had toyed, now a tug of some strength and duration. He suffered in silence. 'Jacob?'

'Reasonably,' he said.

'I wonder what reasonably means.'

'Within reason. Moderately.'

Once again she appeared to change the subject. 'How many others know about Robin and Vera, do you think? There's Jatie for almost sure. Probably the whole tour does.'

'Strikes me as a very close knit community, that tour,' Jacob said. 'And secrets are hard to keep.'

'Secrets are hard to keep,' she said, not in any particular way but as if to reaffirm an abstraction.

'She kissed me,' he said, surprising himself. 'I liked it and didn't break it off as soon as I should have. Also, I was sore at you. Vera, I'm talking about.'

The geography of her face changed. The lines in it deepened, the tiny crescent scar at the corner of her left eye whitened. He braced himself. And she did deliver what he later thought of as the ultimate chest hair wrench, so ferocious he expected to see himself defoliated. It hurt like hell.

But in the aftermath storm clouds seemed to scatter.

'A detached view might be I have mostly myself to blame,' she said.

'No.'

'Yeah, sure, at least in part.'

He was not disposed to argue further. He sensed he had a friend at court and that this friend would work best in a context of silence. He shut his mouth.

'You kept your hands off?'

'I swear.'

'OK then.'

'OK?'

Her own hands moved in slow, annealing circles over the area she had just savaged. 'Better now?'

'The best.'

She kissed his chest, then his nose, and then this and that. He took turns, too, the effect of which was to gather all that was awkward and unyielding between them and deliver it to history—and to delay for a while any further professional discussion.

CHAPTER 7

'Interesting combination, Vera and Robin,' she said. 'They could bust up hearts from either side of the plate, as it were.'

'Could and did,' Jacob said and then thought some more about the intricate and chemically unsound unit lovers formed. It was a high risk venture to come between them. Or, at times, even near them. Like a Sunday stroll in a minefield.

'How long did their affair last?'

'According to Win, it never ended. It just got interrupted from time to time. Robin married Bry, Vera took this lover or that, but these were only interims. She says Vera came to see her a few days after Robin's death. She stayed a week and maybe spoke five words. She just sat in the living-room staring into the fireplace. That's what she was doing when I found her in Bry's apartment, incidentally, just staring into the fireplace.'

'Guilt,' Helen said.

'Or grief.'

'What did it seem like to Aunt Win?'

'She wouldn't put words to it.'

'Listen to me, Jacob, while I put words to it. They had a fight, Robin and Vera. A jealous one. Over Bry maybe. And during it, Vera killed her. Well, it wouldn't have been too hard to do. You put a pillow over your lover's face, and at first, maybe she refuses to believe that what's happening really is. Particularly if there's booze involved. And by the time she comes to realize, she's lost too much strength to do anything effective. I can see that. Theoretically, at least, you can, too.'

'Yes.'

'Jacob, are you still so certain Bry's guilty?'

'I was never certain.'

'But you're less so now than before?'

He lifted her chin and kissed her. But then he shook his head sadly. 'What I'm certain of, my love, is that nobody can be in two places simultaneously.'

'God, you're such a mule. Did I even mention Vera's name? Damn it, Jacob, I don't dislike the woman, not as much as you think I do anyway. All I'm asking you to do is be fair. Grant that things have changed somewhat and keep an open mind. I mean, there are interesting possibilities that aren't named Vera. There's Sherry, for instance, whose feelings for her sister were at the very least ambivalent. There's Jatie with his ancient grudge. And speaking of grudges, how about Hattie Lockridge? And Boswell, of course.'

Which reminded her that Jacob, too, suffered a couple of information gaps. She filled in one of them.

'Interesting,' he said when she was finished.

'If true.'

'Do you believe him?' he asked.

'*You* sound as if you might.'

'Well, as I recall Bry's story, he never actually saw who was in that bedroom. And Robin never actually said.'

She stared at him. 'Oh my God, Vera!'

'Possibly. I don't say for sure, but it could have been.'

Diving back into the Horowitzian forest. 'That's brilliant. I can't stand how brilliant you are sometimes.'

'I try,' he said modestly.

'There's got to be a way. There just has to be. Jacob, you've got to come up with it.'

'What?'

'A way for Vera to be here and there simultaneously. Maybe she's got a twin?'

'She hasn't.'

'Well, then, a first cousin, a double, someone who looks so much like her the two of them have been fooling people for years and years.'

'Maybe.'

'No maybes. It has to be. You know that as well as I do. Swear to me you'll think on it.'

'I'll think, I'll think.'

'And Jacob . . . ?'

'What?'

'Swear you'll never be foolish about Bry Gilchrist any more.'

'I swear.'

'Or about anyone else.'

'Or about anyone else.'

'You're such a liar,' she said contentedly.

In the dining-room the following morning they found Boswell breakfasting alone. He looked up from his newspaper, registered Jacob's presence without undue emotion, and beckoned them to join him. It was off-season. Only a dozen or so guests kept them company in the large, elegant —almost opulent—room, and waiters beamed at them, as if they embodied a chance to justify existences.

'Figured you'd turn up pretty soon,' Boswell said to Jacob as they took seats. And then to Helen, 'Hey, lady, you can fool Tommy Boswell only when you've got him looking the wrong way. I know a team when I see one.'

No corrections or emendations from the Horowitzes. Eager for their breakfasts, they did not yet have their minds on higher things. They sent a pair of intent gazes towards a leggy young person who was reassuringly responsive. She took their orders and then almost at once produced. Juice was quaffed, coffee sipped, and rolls munched, after which conversation could move up from monosyllables.

'Vera's sleeping in this morning?' Helen asked.

'And Sherry's sleeping out,' Boswell said. 'She took off bag and baggage, the concierge informs me, sometime after dinner last night. What'd you do, threaten her with mayhem by tennis ball?' He glanced at Jacob to see if he was in on the joke. Jacob made his face reflect tolerant awareness. 'God, I feel good this morning,' Boswell said. 'New job, new expectations, and it's a beautiful day. Come on, get the grub down and let's go for a walk.'

The grub was got down.

It was as billed, the late winter sun miraculously warming and spirit-lifting. They ambled along under it, following the wooded path that led down to the bay. Birds chatted and some sleek looking squirrels turned out to regard them quizzically.

Jacob, reared in cities, was self-consciously aware of noting the interesting ways of flora and fauna. He called a halt to that and confined himself to sniffing hard at the air. It was good air, authentically bracing.

Helen, the true country girl, had gone on ahead, yielding to some invisible pull, and now they could see her ten yards in front of them sitting at the water's edge, staring out. She looked very beautiful. He didn't know what she was thinking of, but he was certain it was not of murder. He didn't think it was connected to him either. As always, that thought unsettled him.

Boswell had been watching her, too. 'You're lucky,' he said.

'So everybody tells me,' Jacob said.

Boswell grinned shrewdly. 'A nip from the green-eyed monster, right? Well, don't sweat it. It's the price you pay for having that kind of woman.'

Jacob turned to him. 'What kind is that?' he asked carefully.

'Easy there, big fella. The kind a lot of guys want is all I meant. Has its downside though, doesn't it?'

'What doesn't?' But Jacob relaxed.

'Also its terrific side, of course. She's special, that's obvious. I mean, I could never, ever hook up with a broad like that because she'd have me hating myself inside a week. There'd be all this straighten out and live up to your potential business, which'd end by messing me up completely. I know it would. Still, I can see what there is to her.'

Jacob thought for the first time that he could see what there was to Boswell. In the curious way his mind behaved this made him try to see Boswell as a murderer. Not hard at all. The stuff of which superior mercenaries were made, he decided. A tough nut, quintessentially amoral and pragmatic to the core, who could nerve himself to anything if he felt the price was right. But the kind also who would have complex taboos and vaguely chivalric codes of behaviour.

The detective gear having kicked in, Jacob wasted no further time in pushing it towards productivity. 'You ever been in that position?'

'What position?'

'Chasing after a woman a lot of other guys wanted?'

Boswell's eyes turned suspicious. 'Spit it out,' he said.

'I just thought maybe you might want to talk a little about Robin.'

'Why in hell would I?'

Jacob shrugged. They had come to a small cluster of rather wimpish tree-stumps, and he parked himself on one.

'That's going to collapse under you,' Boswell said.

'You never know until you try,' Jacob said. 'Anyway, better a tree-stump.'

'Than a what?'

'Than a what? Let's see. Better than a collapsing bridge, a ladder . . . what else? Anything you put big-time faith in. Did you love her? Robin, I mean.'

'Oh, for God's sake. Look, we're out here on this magnificent day. The sun—'

'Really love her, that is.'

'As opposed to what?'

'*Love* her, not just because she was rich and famous and you could get something out of that, but because she was . . . you word, special. At least to you.'

'Oh, for God's sake.'

'You did,' Jacob said. 'I'd guess you flat out did.'

'Fuck you, Horowitz.' A moment later, however, he said. 'How the hell would you know?'

'I didn't, until you got sore enough to convince me.'

Boswell stared at him. His skin looked paler and his freckles darker than they had a moment ago, as if he'd been struck suddenly by some virulent new form of measles. It occurred to Jacob he might be planning something with those formidably large-knuckled fists that he kept clenching and unclenching. But that passed. Boswell found a neighbouring stump. Jacob noted it was frail as his, but Boswell plunked down on it, not at all gingerly. Clearly, his mind was elsewhere.

'Did you love her?' he said mimicking Jacob. 'Why ask me junk like that? What am I, some kind of philosopher cop like you, Horowitz? All I am is a dumb jerk tennis player.'

'But she was in your blood.'

'Was she? Maybe. If I knew what that meant maybe I could say for sure.'

'If she could drive you crazy that's one of the signs.'

'Yeah, well she could do that, all right,' Boswell said, his voice harsh, his eyes full of memory. But then, having spoken the words aloud, he was instantly affected by them. He blinked, sobered. His expression changed. Everything in it that had been open became guarded, the practised wariness of someone accustomed to traps and snares. 'Hey, what the fuck's going on here? What the fuck are you trying to get me to say? You think I killed her? Come on, don't just sit there like a goddam sphinx, answer me.'

'The thought may have crossed my mind,' Jacob said.

'You know something?'

'What?'

'I don't believe you.'

Jacob kept silent.

'I think you know as well as I do who kissed off Robin.'

'As well as you do?'

'You heard me.'

'But I haven't heard you name a name.'

'And you won't.'

'Because Poppa Boswell sat you down one day and delivered his famous lecture on survival?'

'You got it, Buster. Keep your nose clean. Stick it where it don't belong, and nothing good ever happens, believe me. Just a lot of half-ass fumbling and stumbling around in the dark.'

The last part of that caught Jacob's attention. The words seemed oddly chosen. Also he thought Boswell regretted them.

'Fumbling and stumbling around?' Anyone I know?'

'Everyone you know, Horowitz.'

'So fumblers and stumblers make it OK with you for Robin's murderer to go free?'

Boswell dug a sizeable rock out of the ground and slung it against a neighbouring tree. 'What the fuck do I care?'

Paradoxically (Jacob thought later), that was the moment he experienced the familiar prickling at the back of his neck, the metaphysical shudder that made the work he did so addictive. A vital piece of the puzzle had just clicked into place. It felt terrific.

But there was still pushing to be done.

'You care, all right,' he said. 'You care so much you haven't tapped in yet to how much you do care. Here's your life-story, thumbnail style. Don't get involved, daddy warns. Never, never. And you never do. All over the world, you are very hot stuff, busting hearts right and left. And then along comes this person, with this face, this way of talking and walking. Goodbye, don't-get-involved. Hello, can't-eat-can't-sleep. Incidentally, it's a lucky thing you didn't get cut.'

Startled. 'What?'

'You know, from broken glass. Because when you're cut you leave blood for lab people to have fun with.'

'What the hell are you talking about?'

But he was squirming. To turn the screw, Jacob readied his famous Cheshire-cat grin, which was about half way home when Helen yelled his name. He got up, turned, but not quite in time. He was shoved hard enough to lose his balance and stumble over the tree-stump he'd been sitting on. Flat on his back, he saw Jatie Ramirez with his hands on Boswell's throat—Boswell forced to his knees. He also saw Helen running up the path. Having reassembled himself with optimum speed, he got there first and kicked Jatie's shin. Jatie howled, slackened his grip, after which, very deliberately, Jacob placed the heel of his hand under Jatie's chin and levered him upwards, allowing Boswell to free himself. After which he rammed his knee into Jatie's stomach and was about to do more when Helen pushed him away.

'Quit,' she said.

He nodded, but knew he wouldn't be able to say anything until the red mist behind his eyes had dissipated.

'Do you carry cuffs in your glove compartment?' Helen asked.

He didn't, and she knew he didn't, but he shook his head affirmatively.

'Shall I get them?'

'No,' Boswell said, his voice raspy. 'No cuffs. He's not going to cause any more trouble.'

'You hear that?' Helen said. 'No more trouble from you, Mr Sneaky Pete Ramirez. You understand? Answer.' She nudged him with her toe.

He took a deep, shuddering breath and through this made an acquiescent noise.

She turned to Jacob. 'OK now?'

'OK.'

She studied him, then placed her forehead against his for a moment before backing away.

Boswell bent to Jatie. 'I never bushwhacked you, not once,' he said. 'I swear that's so. The truth is she just plain got tired of you. You said it yourself. Just as she gets tired of everybody. Just as she'll get tired of me in a few months.'

Jatie's gulps for air were proving fruitful. He got to a

knee. 'Hateful bitch,' he said. Then, glancing sharply up at Jacob, he said, 'I hold nothing against you.'

'Wonderful.'

'Once again, she has caused me to behave like a fool, and you stopped me. From that and worse, so I thank you.'

'OK.'

'But if you listen I can tell you things.'

'Tell me what?'

'What a hateful, murdering bitch she is.'

Jacob shrugged. 'That would be a waste of time.'

'It doesn't matter to you? You think it's all right to send an innocent man to gaol and let a murdering bitch go free? I can tell you things about her, things a good detective would want to know. I can tell you she is a vengeance-lover.'

Jacob took Helen's arm, and they started back up the path.

'Wait!'

They stopped.

'I can tell you something else, that she is a woman-lover.'

'Can you tell me how she can be in two places at once?' Jacob asked.

Jatie stared at him. 'Yes, I can tell you that, too.'

'How?'

Suddenly Jatie shot to his feet and in the air made the sign of a huge crucifix. Then, having formed fingers of his right hand into a V, he spat between them. '*Strega! Strega!*' he said, hissing. 'She is a witch.'

BRY REVISITED

Bry heard the special knock he'd taught Sherry, and, opening the door, saw that Win Cantrell was with her. He hadn't set eyes on Win since the day he'd taken up residence in the safe haven she'd arranged for him. Then, under cover of night, she and Mary Alice—whose small, neat house had been conscripted for the purpose—had conducted him here.

'Mary Alice is moving in with me for a while,' Win had said. 'Which will be a comfort, since I haven't been feeling all that perky. So you'll have privacy here. And if you're reasonably discreet, you'll be safe.'

The door had been shut behind him, imprisoning him. That had been almost four weeks ago. Yes, certainly, a very gentle kind of prison, he acknowledged, but a cage is a cage, no matter how velvety its bars.

Studying her now, he thought Win looked drawn. He knew she was seriously ill, but it seemed to him that inroads had been made during that four-week interval. He wasn't able to hide his reaction and was glad she couldn't see it. Sherry did, though. She shook her head warningly, and he nodded to indicate he was now on his guard.

Having brought them into Mary Alice's tidy living-room, he seated them and took his own seat next to Sherry on the sofa. Win was opposite them in the straight-backed chair Sherry had told him she favoured. He reached for Sherry's hand and noiselessly kissed its palm.

'What is it?' he asked.

'The Horowitzes,' Win said at once, a hint of defiance in her voice. 'Plural.'

'Jacob's here, too?'

'He was,' Sherry said. 'He came at Aunt Win's invitation.' She was annoyed and trying not to show how much.

'Where is he now?'

'Back in his natural habitat, I should imagine,' Win said. 'He had some kind of early morning meeting to make, he said. With your mayor, I think. Anyway he left last night.' She paused. 'I'm sorry, Bry, if his visit upsets you. It just seemed to me important that he should know about Vera. And that you would be best served if the information came from me.'

'You could have asked first,' Sherry said.

Win's back, always straight, got straighter. 'I'm not in the habit of asking. I've been a grown woman for some time now, and I do what seems right to me.'

'Yes, of course,' Bry said. 'I was taken by surprise, that's all. And I agree. Coming from anyone else, he might not have believed it. I don't think I would have. God knows what he'll do with the information . . . Jacob is not easy to predict . . . but if it disposes him a little towards my side, that would be a considerable plus.'

'I think he is on your side,' Win said. 'I truly do.'

'All right,' Sherry said, 'but next time please, *please* ask. I know you mean well, you always do, only it's Bry's neck, and he has to have the say.'

'Thank you for "you always do",' Win said stiffly.

But then Sherry was off the sofa and across the room, her head in Win's lap, her arms around her waist. 'Auntie, don't be angry with me. I'm just so scared all the time. And that man is like . . . he's like that detective in *Les Misérables*. Trailing us, following us . . . I know we won't have any peace until . . .' She shivered. 'Anyway, it's being scared that makes me say stupid things. Forgive me, please.'

Stiffness dissolved. Bending over Sherry, Win said, 'Of course I forgive you.'

Pleased at their accord, Bry watched them for a moment and then clapped his hands briskly. 'Here's the position. The position is that the advent of Jacob Horowitz has had the effect of bringing the pot to a boil. Is that what we think?'

Win leaned forward. 'I liked that man. Instinct tells me

Sherry's wrong about him. I really do believe he's disposed to help. But he can't do much for a fugitive. As long as you're on the run his sole job is to bring you in.'

Bry turned to Sherry, taking her hand. He wanted her to understand things words couldn't convey. Never mind that he didn't know precisely what they were. He hoped his flesh knew and that it would find a way to talk to hers.

'Tell me if I should give myself up.'

She bit her lip. She looked haggard, he thought. She could thank him for those dark shadows, for those haunted eyes. What she could not thank him for was anything worth having.

'If I thought you could get on a plane and fly to Never-Never Land—I mean just disappear—I'd tell you to do that,' she said. 'Only they'd find you, wouldn't they?'

'Would you go with me?'

She took his hand to her breast. 'Oh yes. To wherever.'

'Are you really prepared for that?' Win asked. 'To skulk and sneak for the rest of your life?'

'I'm prepared for anything. Anything that gives us a chance, a slim chance, *any* chance of getting free.'

Bry had the feeling Win was studying him. He knew it couldn't be true of course, that blind eyes couldn't see, but they could sear, he thought. They could make laser-like forays into corners he kept hidden even from himself. He got up and went to the liquor cabinet, which Sherry had stocked for him.

'Anyone else? I'm fixing a scotch for myself, Win. Would you like one?'

'No, thank you. What I'd like is to go home now, if Sherry will help me. I said what I came to say, and all at once I'm quite tired.'

Sherry rose and mouthed: 'I'll be back.' Then she gave Win her arm, who used it to lever herself out of her chair. Bry followed them to the door.

'Thanks, Win. For everything. I owe you the world.'

'You owe me nothing. Whatever I've done, I've done because I think Robin would have wanted me to. She was a heedless, helter-skelter girl, but I honestly believe that she loved you, more than she ever did anyone else. And I loved her more than—' She broke off, but after only half a beat—resumed. 'More than I was ever able to make her understand.'

He let them go. He looked down at the glass in his hand, noting to his surprise that it was empty. He refilled it and took the fresh drink back to the sofa where he stretched out, balancing the glass on his chest. He felt drained, slack of muscle, heavy of limb. The room was dark. He chose not to turn on the lamp near his head, however. Perhaps he would fall asleep for a change, he told himself, though he doubted it. Despite fatigue, he felt sharply, everlastingly awake. He thought about the Horowitzes. He thought about a variety of things he wasn't particularly interested in. Then he made himself think about Sherry.

What a blessing she'd been. What an undeserved stroke of luck to find her willing to be part of the disaster his life had become. Willing? Better say adamant, singlemindedly refusing to consider any alternative.

He'd phoned her from somewhere in South Carolina, his fourth night on the run. On impulse. That wasn't quite true. Not really impulse, because he'd been engaged in a long internal battle about whether to do so or not. But he'd believed the battle to be still unresolved when, just like that, he'd found himself in a phone booth.

He'd *needed* to call her. What he needed to know was how she felt about what had happened. No, no, that was absurd. How she felt about *him*. Did she believe he'd killed her sister? The thought that she might tortured him.

'Of course I don't,' she'd said. 'How could I *ever* think such a thing? And nobody else would have either if you hadn't run. Oh, Bry, why on earth did you?'

He tried to explain that to her, made a hash of it, naturally, but somehow she managed to work through the miasma of stammering, inadvertent pauses, and lost syntax to reach understanding. 'God, I wish I were with you now,' she said. 'You sound so terribly lonely. I'd comfort you.'

'You have already.'

And it was true. In some magical way she'd been able to superimpose her view of him on his own, leavening the ugliness, permitting a thin, pale kind of hope to flicker into life.

'Who could have done it?' It burst out of him, the question he put to himself again and again. 'Who could have so cold-bloodedly . . . Is there a way in hell it could have been someone she knew?'

'Yes,' she said grimly.

He had the feeling she wanted to say more, but when he pressed her she evaded.

'Where are you?' she asked.

He told her.

Give me the phone number and stay there,' she said. 'I've had a thought. I'll get back to you as soon as I can.'

Twenty minutes later—having spoken to Win—she was on the phone again. In due course Mary Alice was waiting at a bus stop for a weary, shabbily dressed middle-aged man in a mouse-brown hairpiece. When he arrived she conducted him to his bolt hole.

Now Bry heard Sherry at the door. In a moment she was kneeling at his side. In another, they were tearing at each other's clothes.

'We're getting to fit,' she said afterwards when they lay next to each other on the rug.

'Yes.'

'I don't mean just physically. We're getting to know each other now, Bry. I never thought I'd be much good as a lover. Too shy. But I am good because of you.'

'You're wonderful.'

The clean, fresh smell of her hair was like Robin's, he thought, though he didn't want to. And yet it was true. Her hair did smell like Robin's. Her skin tasted like Robin's. Her . . .He made himself stop.

'What?' Sherry said.

'Nothing.'

'Tell me.'

'We should have happened sooner,' he said.

He moved away from her, pulled some clothes on for warmth, and crossed the room to the window, drawing the curtain back a little so he could see out. The moon, full and bright earlier in the evening, was now cloud-covered. The dark, deserted street seemed as desolate as any of his recent dreamscapes. She padded up behind him, placed her cheek against his back.

'She won't turn loose,' he said, knowing he wouldn't have to explicate for her. 'Asleep, awake, bits and pieces of her appear, like special effects in the movies. I see her eyes. Or her smile. Or an expression on her face I can't really read except it's in some way taunting. And sometimes I just hear her laughing at me.'

He waited for her to speak. It took a while.

'Both of you,' she said coldly. 'You're a pair, both terrific at blasting my life.'

She was at the door. She drew it open and almost got through it, but then she stopped. Shutting it, she collapsed against it. 'You were just going to let me go?'

'Yes.'

'Let me walk out of your life, just like that?'

'I knew you wouldn't make it,' he said bitterly. 'We're both trapped, different traps, that's all. In your way you're as much of a fool as I am.'

To his surprise she smiled. 'I know that,' she said.

When he reached to take back her coat and purse, he was struck by the weight of the latter. He raised an eyebrow. 'What have you got in there?'

'Mad money. A lot of it.'

He looked at her.

'Getaway money if we need it.'

He put coat and purse on the hall table. 'How much?' he asked.

'Oh, hundreds and hundreds,' she said vaguely.

She had returned to the sofa. She sat there staring at her hands, which were on her knees palms up—an odd, graceless position like that of a gawky, vulnerable adolescent. It touched a nerve, and before he knew it something important had broken loose inside him. He heard himself uttering unexpected words.

'I have to tell you something,' he said. 'I can't be lying to you any more.'

Reflexively, her hands came up to shield herself, and though she pulled them down at once, she turned a quarter away from him, as if to make less of a target.

'Before you tell me whatever it is, tell me one other thing first. Do you love me at all?'

'As much as I can.'

'As much as she'll let you?'

He kept silent.

'Are you going to tell me now that you did kill Robin?'

'No,' he said. 'For God's sake, nothing like that.'

Eyes shut, she said something fervent, but too low for him to hear. When she opened her eyes again she said, 'All right, I'm ready now.'

'I made love to her that night,' he said. He paused for a reaction, but she offered none. He continued. 'She was waiting for me, naked, a siren out of an old Greek myth. It was so absurd it would've been funny . . .'

'Except?'

He kept silent.

'Except it got to you.'

'Yes.'

'And so you made love to her.'

'Yes. But only for a little. Very soon I pushed her away.'

'Why should I take your word for that?'

He smiled thinly. 'Medical evidence corroborates. No semen.'

She said nothing. She sat studying those awkward upturned palms as if she saw stigmata there. He dropped to his knees before her.

'She was all over me, Sherry. Like a damn snake as soon as I walked in the door. And she was so sure of herself, so powerful. Nothing could have made her believe I'd be able to resist her. But she was wrong.'

She watched him, slight body stiff with the effort she was putting into listening.

'I don't know where the strength came from, but it was there. I shoved her away from me, back on to the bed.'

'Say it came from me,' she said. And with a quick, cat-like charge she was off the sofa and clinging to him. 'Even if it's not true, say it. Say you saw my face, and it gave you strength.'

'Yes. That's what happened.'

Her arms wound about his neck. She remained still for a while, almost as if she had gone to sleep. But then she left him, returning once more to the sofa where she sat motionless, knees close together, skirt circumspect.

He watched her, waiting. When she didn't speak right away he went to the window again. A wind-tossed trashcan lid was careening crazily down the otherwise empty street, its clatter audible even through layers of glass. He focused on it, watching its dance, listening to the heavy beating of his heart. He didn't know what he was waiting for, or why he was so certain her next words would be fateful.

'Nothing's going to separate us ever again,' she said. 'Nothing. Believe it.'

And suddenly, somehow, he guessed the secret of her purse—that is, he knew there was more than money in it. They stared at each other. He crossed the room to her, crushing her against him.

'Terrible things are not going to happen to us,' he said.

'I know. I won't let them.'

She lifted herself to kiss his mouth, her teeth hurting him. But when she stepped free a moment later a transformation had taken place. She seemed almost relaxed, in a curious way businesslike.

'I do believe a nightcap is exactly what we both need,' she said and briskly set about preparing them. She gave Bry his. 'Now down to cases. Will you meet with Helen?'

'Yes.'

'But not to turn yourself in.'

'I can't. I know that's probably the sensible thing to do, but I can't make myself do it.'

'Of course you can't.'

They were silent a moment. Then he said, 'Helen will help us.'

'Will she?'

He drained his glass and joined her on the sofa. Lifting her chin, he said, 'You don't really know her, so it's hard for you to believe in her.'

'In unswerving loyalty? Yes, you're right. It's hard these days to believe in that.'

'Not just loyalty. In *her*. In what she can do for us.'

'What does that mean?'

He smiled. 'It means she's one of those people who, if she wants to, can make a miracle.'

She poured him an inch more of scotch, clicked glasses, and managed a smile to match his. 'A miracle would be lovely,' she said.

In the dark the porch chairs took on suggestive shapes, and as he waited for Sherry he converted them into lurking animals. It was an old game. As a child he'd played it often —points if he could frighten himself; major points if, having done so, he could restore calm within a reasonable interval. His mouth felt dry. In contrast sweat had gathered under his arms and at the small of his back, despite the chilliness of the night. Stress sweat. It was different, smelled different from good, honest running sweat.

Sherry returned. 'The security guard's checking the parking lot,' she said. 'Come. We'll go up the fire stairs.'

He followed her. She led him to a corridor that circled the lobby like the rim around a wheel until it dead-ended at a glass-topped door. She opened that and waited for him to pass through. A narrow, wooden staircase was revealed. She pointed at it but then changed her mind and held him back so she could precede him. At the top she turned left, stopping at a door about a quarter of the way down the corridor. She looked at him.

'OK?' she said.

'Yes.' They were both whispering.

'It's so strange,' she said. 'As if I'm in a dream.'

'I know.'

Her face broke apart. When the fragments resolved themselves he saw the kind of desperation with which he was only too familiar. He'd been seeing it in the mirror for days. A fox's eyes must glitter like that, he thought, when its field of vision went solid with baying hounds.

But she had, he'd learned, a way of fending off panic. She called on it now, and though she continued to blink much too rapidly, her voice was steady enough.

'Kiss me,' she said.

He did.

She reached up for him again, as if to fasten the first kiss in place. 'I'm ready,' she said. 'If you are, too, knock at the door.'

'Yes,' he said.

And he realized then how excited he was, how much hope he was investing in Helen's magic. He really did believe in it. Helen would shoulder their burden. Somehow she would neutralize the forces arrayed against him. He believed it powerfully. It was important to believe that way—hard, with scrunched-up eyes and nails slicing painfully into palms. Belief like that could unlock closets.

He knocked.

Sherry said, 'Helen . . . ?'

They waited. Nothing. But just as he was about to knock again they heard movement, then Helen's voice.

'Yes?'

She gripped his hand. 'It's me,' she said. 'Sherry.'

Pause. 'Just a second.'

Fifteen, twenty seconds. Or hours, or æons. Sounds of a chain being undone at last. The door was drawn open, but it wasn't Helen who stood there. It was Jacob. Bry tried to run, no use. Jacob caught him easily after a step or two, dragging him into the room, Sherry on Jacob's back, slamming fists into him until Helen pulled her off.

The battle had been intense but quiet, no raised voices. All other doors remained shut. As Jacobs shut *his* door he slung Bry on to the bed and said, 'Stay there.' He turned to Sherry being restrained by Helen. 'Does she have to break your arm?'

'Let her,' Sherry said.

'Sherry,' Bry said softly.

'There's your loyalty,' she said, spitting the words at him. 'You like it? Makes me want to vomit.' But she allowed her shoulders to loosen, and Helen let her go.

Bry looked at Helen. Her face was expressionless, an iron face. He told himself she was dissimulating, a ploy for Jacob's benefit and refused to think beyond that.

Jacob had been saying something. It wasn't until he finished that Bry realized he had been formally arrested for Robin's murder.

'No,' he said anguished. 'Jacob, you can't honestly believe I could have killed her.'

'Can't I?'

His face and Helen's—identical masks, inquisitors' faces. Bry's stomach turned over.

Sherry, bitterly: 'You called yourselves his friends, but you never were, were you? Rats and traitors from the beginning. Everything vile and rotten.'

It's some kind of subtle game, Bry told himself. An intricate and incredibly tricky game, which it would have to be to deceive a man as clever as Jacob. Hope rekindled. If anyone could pull that off, Helen could. Just trust her, he told himself. Just keep your wits about you, and give her a chance to bring you through.

'What I intend to do,' Jacob said, 'is ease you out of here and over to my car, no cuffs, nothing—for friendship's sake. Or you can have the state cops with bells and whistles. Up to you.'

'I'll do anything you want,' Bry said. 'All I ask is that you listen to me a minute.'

'What for?'

'Jacob,' Helen said, 'we'll listen a minute.'

'There's no point to it,' he said, irritated. 'And I'd just as soon not.'

'Is there some reason for godawful hurry that I don't know about?'

He held fire an instant before shrugging. 'All right, we'll listen a minute,' he said.

Bry wet his lips. They felt cracked and swollen, as if blistered by a cruel desert sun. 'I know the evidence is damning. Nobody has to tell me that. And I know you have to take me in. It's your job. But I need a promise from you.'

'What promise?'

'That you won't stop searching.'

'For what? For an honest man?'

'Jacob, for God's sake, I'm innocent.'

Jacob sighed. 'What you are is very damn good. I'm impressed. What you're not is innocent.'

'How can I prove it to you? I mean to you, personally. I'm not talking about a court of law.'

Jacob shook his head. 'Bry, let's go now. It's a long trip, and this isn't doing you any good.'

'Wait. Please.'

Bry shot a look at Helen and caught a flicker of expression. Something meaningful, he thought. Something indicating that if he could give her an opening, any kind, she might make her move at last. Words leaped to his service.

'Jacob, I have to tell you I lied to you before. And to you, too, Helen. I *did* make love to Robin. I said I didn't, but I did. But I swear to you both that's all I've lied about.'

'And the window?'

'The window?' For a moment he had no idea what Jacob was talking about.

Jacob smiled thinly. 'You do have a tough time keeping that window in mind. When you came home from the hospital that night, was the window broken or not?'

Bry stared at him, his mind working frantically. And then suddenly it went deliciously blank, and he wanted to laugh at how blatantly *Lady or the Tiger* the situation had become. Broken. Not broken. Choose one.

'Broken,' he said.

'Life's hard for liars, isn't it? Worse than chess. All that keeping things straight, I mean.'

'*Not* broken,' Bry said. 'It couldn't have been. Jacob, I'm tired. I've been under a . . . Of course the window couldn't have been broken.'

'No, it couldn't have been. Not if Robin was alive when you left the apartment.'

'She was. I swear—'

'Not if it was to be broken by her killer gaining entry, which didn't happen, incidentally.'

'Jacob—'

'Actually, you never saw any broken window. That's why you didn't mention it in your first phone call to me. You didn't mention it because you didn't know there was such a thing until you read about it in the newspapers. Aha, you said then. Neat! A broken window. I can make use of that.'

'That's not true.'

'Tom Boswell broke the window,' Jacob said patiently. 'He went to your apartment, knowing Robin would be there. She'd made no secret of it. What he says is he couldn't sleep, couldn't stop thinking, and couldn't stay away. At any rate, he must have arrived shortly after you took off. He hung around for a minute or two, got even more restless, and decided to sneak a peek. Something about the way Robin was stretched out on the bed made him knock. When she didn't move, he broke in. And it was Boswell of course who called 911.'

'No! He's lying. *He* killed her. He got there *before* I left. When he saw me go he broke in to confront her. They had a lovers' quarrel, and he put that pillow over her face and kept it there until every spark of life was choked out of her. And *then* he called the police to place the blame on me. He's—'

'Stop it, Bry,' Helen said.

He looked at her. Not a trace of iron there now, a face full of pity.

'Boswell's lying, Helen,' Bry said. 'He was jealous, insanely jealous. Jacob, you have to get hold of him. You have to pressure him, scare him into admitting the truth.'

'You're a wonder, pal.'

'Jacob, could I cold-bloodedly kill? It's *me* I'm asking about. Your friend, Bry Gilchrist, not some stranger. For God's sake, answer!'

'Cold-bloodedly is not the issue, is it? Cold blood doesn't enter into it. But I'll tell you what does. It's that you lie so much.'

Bry shut his eyes and took a deep breath. 'All right,' he said. 'I did lie about the window. How can you blame me for that? It was a chance to . . . I mean, there was so *much* going against me. But I am *not* a murderer. I'm not. I couldn't be.'

Jacob kept silent.

'How disgusting you are.' It was Sherry, shaking her head in the same kind of disbelief she might have accorded the unlooked-for appearance of something primordial and slimey. 'I just wonder how you can live with yourself. You know who the real killer is. The whole world does. And you stand there playing out this awful charade.'

Jacob turned to her. 'Who's the real killer? Vera?'

'Monsters. The pair of you.'

'Vera Menchicov's the real killer?'

She glared her fury. 'You *know* she is.'

As if wearied by a refrain gone stale, Jacob said, 'Nobody can be in two places at the same time.' But when he turned back to Bry his voice was gentler. 'Nobody can, Bry. I kept trying to figure a way around that, but there isn't any. It's just one of those immutable truths.'

But Bry was no longer listening, not to Jacob. He sat at the edge of the bed, covering his face, trying to disconnect from everything in the room. Something was at the edge of his consciousness. He could sense it there, though it was without definition. It was like something shrouded in fog —a form indefinable and yet familiar. Familiar, yes, for now he could hear its hateful, taunting voice.

'Maybe you don't want to fuck, Bry, because you *can't* fuck. Maybe that thing of yours has shrivelled into a tiny, curly—'

And then grabbing the pillow to cut off the nastiness. He

could remember that, yes. But surely he had released her. Of course he had. It simply wasn't in him to have done anything else.

Jacob took his arm. 'It's time, Bry.'

'I didn't kill her,' he said. 'I couldn't have. Some people can, some can't, and killing just isn't in me. Yes, I put the pillow over her face. I can see myself doing that now, but that was merely to ... I let her go. Of course I did. For God's sake, Helen, ask yourself—how could I have killed her and not remember it?'

The logic of that seemed compelling to him, but Helen, her voice unequivocal, said, 'I don't know, Bry, but you did.'

He stared at her, stunned.

Jacob's grip on his arm tightened.

'Let him alone,' Sherry said, and when they turned to her they saw what had given the words such authority. The small, snub-nosed revolver was pointed at Jacob. 'Let him go and back off. I'll shoot if you don't. I mean that.'

To Bry, she appeared transfigured, exaltation shining in her eyes, her face pale, abstracted. He thought—resisting it at first because it seemed so alien—that she was enjoying herself. But then he knew he was right. She had prepared herself for this, waited patiently for her moment, and now it was here. She was the quintessential martyr, alight at the approach of fulfilment. He knew she would shoot.

'Bry, we're leaving,' she said.

'No, you're not,' Jacob said.

'You're going to try to stop me? Oh, how I hope you do.'

'Jacob,' Helen said urgently, 'don't be a fool. Let them go for now.'

But he took a step forward. As he did the gun came up a little higher, held a little steadier, Bry thought.

'You're wrong,' Sherry said as if in reply to something she read in Jacob's face.

It was then that Helen and Bry made simultaneous leaps —she towards Sherry, he to a point between Sherry and Jacob. She arrived a split second late.

But Bry got there in time.

EPILOGUE

The National Tennis Center
Flushing Meadow, NY
September, 1993

'Shot to remember, Freddie Jo,' Skip said as the delighted crowd roared its approval.

'When you're loose, you're loose,' she said. 'You'll try any silly shot—and make it. Let's watch the replay.'

'All right, there it is,' Skip said. '*Just* out of reach. Wow, what's the percentage on a half volley number like that?'

'Nil, or next to it. What she should have done, of course, was hit deep as she could, then scramble to get back in position. Still, Vera's one of those players hooked on brilliance. It's both her strength and her weakness. And right now she's in a zone.'

'And poor Hattie's in a pit,' Helen said, returning from the kitchen as instant replay again showed dinked ball eluding desperately outstretched racket. She handed Jacob his coffee mug and sat on the floor, her back against the sofa on which he sprawled.

'Deep, deep in the pit and looking up at the handwriting on the wall,' she added boldly mixing her metaphors.

'She's only behind one service break in this set,' Jacob pointed out.

'Another on the way. You can see it in her shoulders.'

'You can see it in Hattie's shoulders,' Freddie Jo said. 'They're beginning to sag.'

'That Freddie Jo,' Helen said, tapping her head. 'All brain. Perceptive as hell.'

But Hattie's next serve seemed to belie dire predictions. It was out of a cannon, to Vera's forehand. In reaching it, Vera was pulled far off court, and her return floated to the net, hovering there, a classic sitter. Hattie, hungry, stormed in, set herself, took aim and blasted her overhead a foot beyond the baseline.

The umpire signalled out, no news to anyone in that suddenly hushed arena.

'Oh my,' Skip said.

'Three-love,' Freddie Jo said, knell-like. 'Down a set and two service breaks. A long, long way for Hattie to climb back.'

'Perceptive she may be,' Helen said, 'but I don't care much for Freddie Jo.'

'Why not?'

'She's one of those who loves doom and downfall. I can tell.'

'How? She's your basic deadpan.'

'Right. And that's how you tell.'

He was about to grin and bring shamans and/or totems into the conversation but stopped himself when he saw that her own face had gone bleak. She rose, crossed the room, and turned off the TV set.

He looked at her.

'All of a sudden I feel antsy. Antsy as hell, Jacob, and I need you.'

She hurried up the steps to their bedroom.

They made love, but after that he said, 'You were thinking about Bry, weren't you?'

'I was not.'

He rolled a tendril of her hair around two of his fingers.

She sighed. 'All day long I've been feeling rotten about him. Don't ask me why today because I can't explain it. Maybe it's the tennis, which would be ironic, wouldn't it, since he never cared for it all that much. Still, there it is. I can't get him out of my mind. Sorry.'

He kept silent.

'Don't be angry.'

'I'm not. He's dead, and I'm here holding you.'

She took his hands and pressed them against her breasts, but it was a loving not a lustful gesture. He guessed that they were not yet finished with Bry, and he was right.

'Jacob, I really do think he blocked it out . . . or disconnected . . . or however you want to say it . . . the actual killing, I mean. Maybe that was the only way he could live with it, as an act perpetrated by someone who wasn't him.

I spoke to Kathy Peterson, the psychiatrist at the hospital. She says it's possible. She says that when it happens it's something called acute non-psychotic syndrome.'

'Or hysterical amnesia.'

'Or hysterical amnesia, right. She says, for instance, that serial killers disconnect that way.'

'Yes.'

'Yes what?'

'Yes, I know that about serial killers.'

'But that's not what I'm asking.'

'I know that, too.'

'Damn you, Jacob, what I'm asking for the half-dozenth time is if *you* think it's what Bry did. And please, please don't tell me again that you don't know.'

'I don't.'

'I could easily grow to hate you,' she said.

'Could you?'

'No.'

'But she got back a little of her own by stroking that patch towards the back of his head where the hair was definitely losing to bald. He pushed her hand away.

'And I've been feeling rotten about Sherry, too,' she said. 'She just sits and stares. Jacob, will she ever come out of that hospital?'

'What does Dr Peterson say?'

'She says it's too early to tell. There's so much shock and trauma involved that it's like the Sherry essence is buried alive. She says you just have to wait and see. And find ways not to lose hope.'

'Sounds like a smart lady.'

'What Dr Peterson says about you, Jacob—that smart lady, I mean—is that you ought to go and see Sherry. Not for her, you know. For you.'

He nodded.

'Unfinished business causes stomach problems.'

He smiled. 'Which is that, a Dr Peterson diagnosis or a Helen Horowitz one? I lost track.'

'Will you go?'

'I guess I better.'

She kissed him. He held her and neither spoke for a while until, suddenly, she shivered, gooseflesh pimpling arms and shoulders.

'What? What?' he asked.

'That damn Bryant. I mean, no matter how he tried to hide from it, the fact is he adored her. And he killed her. How could he have?'

Jacob sighed. 'Because he wanted to. That's why people always do what they do, because they want to. Never underestimate the power of desire, my old grandpa liked to say. Desire, it's the lion of motivations.'

'I wish your old grandpa were here right now.'

'Me, too. Maybe you'd cut me some slack.'

'So I could ask him *why* Bry wanted to kill her.'

'Why? Why? You always want explanations. Maybe there *is* no explanation. Maybe not everything can be explained.'

'It's just that we're all capable of killing?'

'Maybe.'

'Given the right set of circumstances anybody and everybody can kill.'

'Maybe.'

'Could you kill me?'

'No.'

Small-voiced, she said, 'How can you be sure?'

He remembered the quote and paraphrased it. 'Because the Everlasting has fixed his canon 'gainst self-slaughter.'

She went absolutely still. He brought her closer to him, thinking that only she could dispel movement that way, in effect freezing time. It was the Indian in her, he told himself and smiled self-mockingly, aware that this was his catch-all for whatever she did that mystified him. And aware, also, that he employed it often.

But then, a moment later, she was out of bed and turning on the television set—just as Hattie Lockridge slammed a backhand down the line and threw her racket in the air triumphantly.

The crowd erupted. Freddie Jo and Skip jabbered at each other excitedly, and it was clear the match was over. Doomed Hattie had somehow won.

Helen stared at Jacob as if this required interpretation, as if more were involved than the mere ending of a tennis match, as if that rifled backhand and God's design for the world were somehow inextricable. It was an accusing stare. And peremptory, too, in its demand for response.

'Go figure,' Jacob said mildly.